BRADLEY'S BRIDE

SEVEN BRIDES FOR SEVEN BROTHERS
BOOK TWO

KATHLEEN LAWLESS

ISBN ebook: 978-0-9937701-8-0

ISBN print: 978-1-989873-50-2

Seven Brides for Seven Brothers Reviews

What reviewers are saying about the *Seven Brides for Seven Brothers* series...

"GREAT SERIES!!!" Top 500 reviewer

"If you have not picked up the series, do yourself a favor, you will be glad you do."

"I loved the continuity in the series—and the resolution"

"Sweet and romantic."

"This entire series is going into my library to be read again and again."

"I just love reading Kathleen's books—they keep me coming back for more."

If you haven't already done so, sign up for my VIP Reader's Newsletter and be the first to hear about free books, fan-priced sales, and my new series. Details at the end of the book.

CHAPTER 1

W hat a beautiful day for a wedding! Amanda was so excited she could barely keep still as her best friend, Laura, exchanged vows with Brody Mason. Laura looked radiant, literally glowing from within, a beacon of happiness Amanda saw mirrored on the groom's face.

As she shifted her gaze from Brody to his six brothers lined up alongside him, her eyes lingered on Bradley, third from the end, next to the twins. Other than the twins, the men weren't brothers by blood, but she'd seen them often enough to know a deep bond connected all seven.

The reverend's voice interrupted her perusal. "I now pronounce you man and wife. You may kiss the bride."

Laura turned and passed Amanda her bouquet just before Brody gathered his bride close for the wedding kiss. Amanda sighed at the sheer romanticism of the day. As she sighed, her mind skipped back to that secret and joyful place. A magic evening here at the Copper Moon Ranch, and the dances she had shared with Bradley.

In typical male fashion, he had avoided her ever since.

The wedding proceeded as weddings were wont to do,

with good-natured jokes and ribbing toward the groom from his bachelor brothers. Laura was new in Bullet, but the Masons were well-liked. Thanks to generous friends and neighbors, a long trestle table was heaped with innumerable plates and bowls of food, enough to feed a small army.

Amanda watched the gracious way Laura flitted from guest to guest, thanking them for coming. A keg of beer had been tapped and its consumption among the gents added to the buzz of merriment floating through the air. A four-piece group of musicians began warming up on the make-shift stage and dance floor to the left of the barn.

Amanda circled the ranch's many guests, wondering how she could feel so lonely in the midst of a party. Her life as an only child had always felt pretty solitary with only her and Ma. Living in a small town in the shadow of Yuma, Arizona, Amanda told herself she preferred the small-town life. But how could she be sure when that was all she knew? She'd been feeling restless for a while now, harking back to the first day she met Laura.

On the far side of the dance floor she saw Bradley standing alone, his face in shadow. Perhaps he felt as lonely as she did, part of the revelry but never really belonging. One more thing they had in common.

From a practical side, she knew it was silly of her to hope he thought of her as often as she thought of him. But she had seriously hoped that on the day of the wedding, wearing her fancy bridesmaid dress in a flattering shade of apricot that did wonderful things to her skin tone, with her auburn hair curled and twined through with flowers, that she might at least have merited some attention from him, if not a dance or two.

She was gathering her courage to approach him, suggest they share a dance like they had once before, when there was a frantic clang of spoons against glassware, a signal for the newlywed couple to exchange a kiss, followed by whistles and catcalls.

Smiling as the newlyweds complied, she nearly missed seeing Bradley disappear into the barn. Before she had a chance to talk herself out of it, she set her glass down and followed.

She wasn't overly surprised by Bradley's destination. Somehow, she instinctively knew he preferred the company of animals over humans. As Bullet was too small to have a fulltime vet, Bradley often helped out nearby ranchers when they had an animal in distress.

The barn's interior was dim, the only illumination from the lanterns outside, the air peppered with the smell of hay and warm animal flesh. As she walked past the shadowy stalls and heard the occasional snuffle or stirring of sleeping animals, her feet made no noise against the straw-strewn floor.

She heard Bradley before she saw him. Caught the low murmur of his voice as he soothed an agitated mare in a nearby stall. She saw him crouch down and run a large, capable hand up the mare's front leg as he spoke in low, soothing tones. Amanda stood still as stone, envying the bond between man and beast. The moment was both intimate and poignant.

Suddenly, aware she was intruding, she spun to leave, but the hem of her gown caught against a nearby pitchfork and sent it clattering to the ground. Bradley bolted upright. Their gazes met.

"What are you doing here?"

Amanda opened and closed her mouth several times but couldn't seem to find any words.

She cleared her throat and tried again. "Maybe I was

looking for you." She shocked herself with the boldness of her tone, never mind the way she sashayed toward him as if she'd been doing it her entire life, taking her cue from the professional ladies she'd seen in town.

"Maybe I was remembering how well we moved together on the dance floor that night Laura was rescued. Wondering what else we might do well together."

Merciful heavens! Was that her speaking? She sounded like a total hussy. His eyes on her were dark, unfathomable, giving away nothing. Was he intrigued? Or repelled by her forwardness?

"I'm going to do us both a favor and forget what you just said."

When he made to brush past her, almost as if she didn't exist, Amanda couldn't help herself. "Bradley, I—" She reached for him, caught the sleeve of his formal linen shirt.

"Don't!"

One word.

Dismissive.

Final.

Before she had a chance to reply, their exchange was interrupted by a ruckus outside. She started at the sound of shots being fired, followed by a mass cry of terror. They both dashed toward the door of the barn as more shots rang out.

Bradley pushed her behind him as he grabbed a rifle near the doorway. He emerged from the barn with Amanda on his heels. At least a dozen horses and riders raced through the property.

She covered her mouth in wordless horror as wedding guests shrieked and scattered for cover. Laura raced toward Amanda and Bradley, trying not to stumble on the hem of her wedding dress. One of the riders cut and veered toward her, cutting her off. He slowed down just enough to drop a misshapen bundle at her feet. Amanda could just make out what he said to Laura over the commotion.

"Little wedding gift, Mrs. Mason. Even though I'm hurt I wasn't invited."

Amanda held her breath as, taking careful aim, Bradley got off a shot that appeared to clip the man. The man's horse reared as he sawed on the reins and turned the other way, straight toward the dance floor. The musicians grabbed their instruments and scattered.

The intruders, all of whom wore bandannas shielding their features, were riding in circles, firing shots into the air, yelling and hooting. Brody raced to the side of his bride who stood frozen, staring in horror at the bundle at her feet. Abruptly, there was a volley of shots from just over the rise.

Now who was shooting? Amanda stuck to Bradley like a burr, grateful for his size. His strength. The way he made her feel safe. Another round of bullets sent the riders scattering back the way they'd come, laughing in merriment as they rode away down the driveway.

The whole incident felt like it lasted hours but was probably over in minutes. Slowly the guests emerged from where they had taken cover. Obviously shaken, the musicians regrouped and picked up where they had left off playing. As the music resumed, along with a sense of normalcy, people started to pick up scattered plates of food and right knocked-over chairs.

Amanda turned to Bradley, who still held the rifle gripped tightly in one hand. "Hawkes?"

Bradley didn't answer. He strode toward Brody and Laura. Amanda followed. It appeared as if Brody was trying to get Laura to move but she just shook her head.

As Amanda drew closer, her stomach lurched when she saw a cat's gray tail poking out of the cloth bundle that had been dropped near Laura. Her friend's eyes were bright with unshed tears. As Brody attempted to comfort his new wife, Bradley dropped to his knees and scooped up the offending item.

He rose and turned to Amanda. "Killing a defenseless creature has always been Hawkes's signature." Bradley's mouth grew tight. "Heard he was out of jail, got off scot-free for killing his wife. Expect this is his way of letting us know he's not easing up. And neither will we."

Bradley went back into the barn and came out with a shovel.

Amanda thought about the map she had received from her mother shortly before that woman's death. The map that almost got Laura killed.

Her mother had intimated as long as Amanda had it in her possession, it would keep her safe from Hawkes. What Amanda wanted was for her friends, the entire town, to be safe from Hawkes. The fact that he was back on the loose meant no one was safe.

She exchanged a glance with Laura, who appeared to have recovered remarkably quickly. It wasn't that long since Hawkes had tried to kill her friend, but Laura had proven nothing would get in the way of her future with Brody.

"Come and help me reassure the guests. That man will not ruin the most important day of my life." As Laura held a hand her way, Amanda wished for some of her friend's sure-fire confidence.

QUIETLY AND QUICKLY BRADLEY DUG A SHALLOW grave for Smoky the cat, away from the festivities of the wedding. He was grateful for the physical exertion as he tumbled the small, cloth-covered body into the grave and shoveled sandy dry soil overtop. It also got him away from the wedding and all the temptations that came with the day. Including Amanda.

Smoky wasn't the first dead animal he'd buried and wasn't likely to be the last. From a young age he'd found it easy to love animals of every species. Simple creatures that loved you back unconditionally. Humans were a whole different tangle.

He cared deeply for his adopted family, all of them, but he couldn't profess to love them. Maybe because the woman who gave him birth hadn't loved him enough to keep him, but had dumped him on some church steps like unwanted trash.

Passion he understood, in all its many guises— a heated moment of anger or lust, longing or fear. Along with hatred. Hatred was easy. Hatred for the sadistic beasts who ran the orphanage where he grew up. Hatred for the farmer who beat him on a daily basis until he ran away. Hatred for Hawkes and his killing, thieving, terrorizing ways like tonight.

The urge to protect beat strongly in his chest. The weak, the vulnerable, the women and children who couldn't protect themselves. And Amanda. In order to protect her he had to stay away. To protect her from himself.

He'd seen the way she looked at him, trust and longing in her gaze. He never should have danced with her that night. It had been a weak moment. One he was now regretting. Witness her actions earlier. How could he make her see he was no good for her? No good for anyone.

He'd stick around till Hawkes was dealt with once and for all. Then he'd be on his way. That was his way. The only way.

The bleakness of the future welled up into that dark hole inside him and settled there with a thud. Echoed by the shovelfuls of dirt that he heaped on the tiny grave.

"READY TO GO, MISS COOKE?" Ian Northrup, a recent visitor to Bullet stood nearby, holding his hat. Around them, the remnants of the wedding celebration were all packed away. The musicians were gone. The last lingering guests were getting ready to depart.

"Thank you for waiting," Amanda said. Not even to herself would she admit she'd been lingering, hoping to see Bradley before she left. Hoping ... Hoping what?

Pasting on a smile she was far from feeling, Amanda clambered up beside Ian Northrup in his rented rig.

"Trust my brother-in-law to disrupt things tonight," Ian said darkly as their conveyance started to roll.

Amanda nodded. Most of the town had been hoping Hawkes would stay locked up for a good long time. "It's a shame he got off for killing his wife. I mean your sister," she added hastily. No one held it against Northrup that his sister had made the ill-fated decision to marry Hawkes decades earlier.

"I only wish I'd made it back sooner," Ian said. "I could have saved Ann, if I wasn't so bent on improving my own fortunes."

She patted his hand. "No one knows that for sure." Ian had had his dead sister's remains exhumed to discover signs of arsenic poisoning before she drowned, but not even that finding was enough to keep Hawkes locked away for any amount of time.

Amanda was dead certain it was not the first time

Hawkes had gotten away with murder but kept her suspicions to herself. Northrup wasn't from these parts and was likely to soon be gone, back to wherever he called home.

AMANDA SAT AT THE PIANO, her fingers motionless atop the keys. Lately, the house seemed too darn quiet, taking all the heart out of her playing. Life had been so fun and full and busy when Laura lived here. First came the Mason boys, swarming around like bees, all pretending to woo her friend in an effort to shake some sense into Brody.

Then the excitement of helping rescue Laura, followed by the party at the Copper Moon to celebrate Bradley's birthday. She sighed at the memory of that night, the dances she had shared with Bradley. The way his hands had cinched around her waist, pulling her close as he smiled down at her, his dark eyes warming her right to the tips of her toes.

Even now, remembering that night, she felt a rush of heat that had nothing to do with the outside temperature and everything to do with Bradley. She hadn't seen him much while the preparations were under way for Laura's wedding to Brody. When they weren't herding cattle, all the brothers kept busy building Brody and his intended a new house on the ranch.

She rose and selected a book from the bookshelf, then flipped it open to reveal the hollowed-out center. Secreted inside was the envelope from her mother. She fingered the yellow edges of the confession signed by her father before he disappeared, the disintegrating edges of the red bandanna from his outlaw days, and the faded map. Laura had tried to follow the markings on the map and it had nearly gotten her killed. Would Hawkes come after Amanda if he knew she had this in her possession?

After the disruption of the wedding, she doubted the papers inside were safe where they were. Best she move them. She glanced to the window. Outside, dusk began to cloak their small town. It was time she got ready for work.

By the time she left, her own mother wouldn't have recognized her. She tugged a blonde curl of the wig so it ringed a heavily rouged cheek. Covering her head and shoulders with a light shawl, she made her way to the newly-opened "fancy ladies'" house on the outskirts of town. The proprietress, Zara, operated out of Yuma but had recently started sending several of the girls to work in Bullet a few nights a week.

The churchgoers of Bullet would be shocked if they knew how their pianist earned the money to keep a roof over her head and food on the table. The tunes she played in the front parlor of the brothel were a far cry from Sunday hymns. But the tiny wage, coupled with the generosity of the patrons as they filled her tip jar, meant she could continue to live independently, pretending her mother had left her well provided for, without dipping into the "blood money". Amanda refused to touch the cache left behind by her outlaw father, convinced it was tainted.

When a newcomer entered the parlor, her heart quickened, then sank. Quickly, she looked away. It shouldn't be a total surprise to see Bradley frequent the establishment, for she had seen some of the other Mason boys here upon occasion. They weren't regulars, which led her to believe they mostly made the trip to Yuma for their gentlemanly entertainment.

Given the other women present in their skimpy attire, no one ever had eyes for the pianist, and Amanda preferred it that way. Bradley didn't linger, just voiced his preference for one of the new girls and took her upstairs. Poor thing looked young and scared. Amanda hoped Bradley would be gentle with her.

Normally Amanda stayed until the house grew quiet, but tonight her fingers fumbled so often that the woman in charge sent her home early, casting her a pitying look. Were her feelings so obvious?

Normally Amanda was not nervous walking home alone this late, but something about tonight felt different, with the echo of muffled sounds in the dark. At first she assumed it was all part of her overactive imagination, conjuring up the stealthy but steady sound of footfalls behind her. She'd walked home alone in the dark many evenings and not felt this sense of unease. Which could have something to do with Hawkes and his ruffians terrorizing the wedding at the ranch.

Someone was definitely behind her. When she lengthened her stride, it sounded as if the person behind followed suit. She turned the final corner, relieved to see the welcome shadow of her modest home. Almost there. And so was her pursuer! She felt his breath, smelled liquor.

"Amanda!" He barked out her name.

He knew who she was!

She started to run, only to find herself caught and held from behind. She struggled to get away. Why hadn't she bought a pistol and learned to use it? She felt the heat of his breath in her ear.

"Be still. It's Bradley."

"Bradley." Her struggles ceased. She had spent many a night imagining his arms around her, but not like this. Tonight, there was nothing gentle or tender in the way he held her. She pushed him away.

"What happened to your little companion for the evening? Done with her so quickly?" She couldn't keep the bitterness from her tone. She had no desire to be Bradley's fancy woman, which appeared to be the only use he had for the fairer sex.

Bradley glanced over his shoulder. "Not out here."

Amanda arched a brow. "If you think for one second that I'm about to invite you inside, you're mistaken. My reputation would be in tatters in minutes."

"Kind of the same as if people find out about your sideline?"

Their eyes warred, his dark and unreadable in the pale moonlight. "All right," she said reluctantly. "But only for a minute."

She approached the front door, key in hand, with Bradley close behind, before she stopped. A sense of uneasiness crept up her spine to lodge at the base of her skull. She felt prickles on the back of her neck at the sight of the door standing slightly ajar.

She had locked it when she left.

CHAPTER 2

B radley must have seen her hesitation.

"Wait!" He stood so close behind her she could feel his body heat warm her to the core. His breath tickled the back of her neck, and beads of perspiration dewed her hairline beneath the wig. She felt rather than saw him draw his gun. Heard the overloud click as he readied the weapon.

Amanda stepped aside as he shouldered his way into the house ahead of her, then followed. She waited just inside the entrance as Bradley checked the other rooms, even though she could tell immediately whoever had broken in was long gone. With unsteady hands, she moved to the table, lit the lantern and adjusted the wick.

Her stomach heaved. The place was in shambles. Books had been ripped from the shelves and tossed about. Feathers spilled from gaping wounds in the cushions on the settee. Pictures had been ripped from the walls. Her home, her refuge, had been violated.

Bradley returned to her side and picked up a book that lay open in the middle of the table. The secret compartment yawned emptily. He turned to her, an expression on his face she'd not seen before. Pity or sympathy, neither of which sat well with her.

"Did they find what they were after?"

She all but fell, weak-kneed, into the closest chair and started to shake.

Bradley stomped into the kitchen and returned holding a glass with a small measure of amber liquid which he put into her hand. "Drink this. It'll help with the shock."

The brandy burned the back of her throat and she coughed, then obediently drained the glass.

"You didn't answer my question."

BRADLEY WATCHED the color slowly seep back into Amanda's pale cheeks, a direct result of the brandy. She gulped in a few deep but shaky breaths. Even though she was barely recognizable in the stupid wig and garish makeup, he kicked himself for not realizing it was her playing the piano at the house. She stared at the empty glass as she turned it around and around in her right hand, no doubt a ploy to avoid making eye contact with him. And who could blame her?

Slow anger roiled in his gut as he glanced around at the destruction done to her home. He and his brothers had sworn to do whatever it took to cut Hawkes down, to destroy him bit by bit. What they hadn't counted on was other folks getting caught in the crossfire.

First had been Laura, nearly killed by Hawkes. And now this.

How many other people's lives would be disrupted before that man was stopped once and for all? He and the others might have breathed a collective sigh of relief when

Hawkes was arrested for the murder of his wife, despite being disappointed it wasn't them taking Hawkes' down.

Not one of them was even a bit surprised when Hawkes beat the charges.

He removed his hat and ran a hand through his thick, dark hair which he knew, together with his coal-black eyes, hinted at a possible Mexican heritage. The abusive farmer who had adopted him was fond of calling him a greaser, minutes before he took off his belt and beat Bradley sense-less over some imagined misstep around their dirt-poor farm.

"That girl tonight." He didn't know why he felt compelled to explain, but he did. "She's friends with Miss Dolly and hates Hawkes nearly as much as I do. She keeps me informed with little snippets she picks up from Dolly. Lets us know what Hawkes is up to."

Amanda seemed fascinated by the wood grain in the tabletop. "Why should I care?"

"I'm hoping you'll trust me. Enough to tell me what you have that Hawkes is so hell-fired to get his hands on."

"What makes you think I have anything of interest to that cretin?"

He crossed his arms over his chest. "Seems pretty clear." He waved a hand to encompass the room in shambles. "This mess. Laura's confrontation with Hawkes, due to some information she gleaned from you. Certain things Dolly overheard Hawkes talking about to a couple of his henchmen."

He watched Amanda deflate further. She tugged off the blond wig and instantly looked more like herself with her ginger curls revealed. "That girl tonight. Is she really your confidante?"

"Why do you think I'm here?" He watched fresh color

spill onto her cheeks. One more time she avoided his gaze. Oh no. Did she think he was here because he fancied her?

He leaned forward in his most aggressive pose. "I heard tonight that Hawkes was bucking for something you have. Possibly handed down from your mother to you?"

"My mother passed away recently." She stated it matter-of-factly.

"And now that Hawkes is no longer behind bars, he's taking care of old business. Whatever your mother had and gave to you, he wants it."

"He didn't get his hands on it," Amanda said flatly.

"You sure?" He nudged the book cover with its secret hidey-hole.

"Red herring," Amanda said. "The real documents are safe."

Bradley stood. Clearly it would take some time for Amanda to trust him. No time like the present to start earning that trust. "Got a broom?"

IT WAS MUCH LATER by the time Amanda stood at the wash basin in her room, scrubbing at her make-up with a face flannel until her lightly freckled complexion was once more her own. With Bradley's help, the house had been more or less put to order. Feathers and broken dishes swept into the trash. Books replaced on the shelves. Furniture righted.

How bitter-sweet to have Bradley working alongside her, knowing he was there not because he cared about her, but because of the documents she had at hand. Well, at waist anyway. Slowly she turned to the bed and began to remove the layers of her clothing until she was down to her underpinnings. Secured near her waist with a myriad of satin fastenings was the cursed envelope with its damning contents. Something she was starting to wish she had never laid eyes on.

She had thought the contents would be safe on her person. Now she wasn't so sure. Whoever broke into her house tonight had the phony envelope she had hidden. How long before Hawkes realized it was just that? A fake.

At least the thieves hadn't found the stash of gold and jewelry hidden beneath a floor board in her room. The jewelry contained a one-of-a-kind necklace rumored to have been stolen from a wealthy socialite during a stage coach robbery. Amanda didn't know the law but she assumed that the piece, coupled with her father's confession and the red bandanna, was enough to implicate Hawkes as the ringleader of Red's Rowdies.

But what of the map Laura had taken and tried to follow? What was hidden on the Masons' ranch that Hawkes didn't want found? Or was Hawkes also looking for something?

Sir Percy Bloom claimed to be in Bullet searching for a boat filled with a fortune in black pearls somewhere on the Copper Moon Ranch. What other secrets remained hidden somewhere on the ranch?

These questions continued to plague her over the next few days as she rehearsed with the church choir. Christmas was fast approaching and they had a number of new hymns to practice.

Home after one particularly long rehearsal, she squealed in delight when she opened the door to a light knock and saw Laura. Her friend wore a newly-married glow of love and contentment. "I've missed you so much." Amanda grabbed Laura in a close hug. "I wasn't sure how long it was appropriate to leave a newly married couple to their own devices before company descended."

Laura colored prettily. "We had a lovely time together before Brody got restless. There's always so much to do on the ranch and even though he knows the others are capable, he still can't resist checking on things." Her tone grew serious. "I heard you had a break-in."

Amanda nodded. "Not the last, I fear, until Hawkes gets his hands on what he thinks I have in my possession."

"A shame he got off for killing his wife."

"Not to mention trying to kill you," Amanda said.

"It was his word against mine. He's very good at persuading others to see things his way."

"And pay off the prosecutor," Amanda added darkly. She knew Laura had worked with those tasked to uphold the law, only to be disappointed when all charges against Hawkes were eventually dropped.

Small consolation that the man had spent a relatively short time in jail. For which he no doubt blamed Laura and the Masons.

"Let's not talk about Hawkes." Laura removed her hat and gloves as Amanda set out the tea things. "Can I help?"

Amanda brushed her away. "You're my guest."

"Not that long ago I was your boarder." Her tone grew serious. "When I lived here, I never realized you worked some evenings."

"Bradley told you."

"He thought I should know. He had no idea who to share the information with, but he didn't want to be the only one who knew. Just in case ..." Her words trailed off.

"In case I don't arrive home one evening?" Amanda asked.

"Something like that."

Amanda rose and busied herself making the tea. "I need the money," she said flatly, as she brought the pot to the table. "Folks think Ma left me well-off, but the truth is her sanatorium stay mostly wiped that out years ago." Other than seeing to her mother's comfort, she refused to touch anything she believed to have been stolen. "There's a bit of gold and jewelry she left, but I believe it's complicit in the robberies."

"Evidence!" Laura's eyes brightened.

"One can hope."

"I admire your determination to be independent, but I was wondering. Is there something else you would rather be doing?"

Amanda rolled her eyes. "You're trained as a school teacher. All I know is how to play the piano."

"But," Laura probed as she stirred her tea to cool it, "in a perfect world, what would you be doing?"

Married to Bradley.

Amanda dismissed the thought before it could even settle. She propped her chin on one hand and stared into space. "Open a music school. Start a dance hall. Direct an opera. There's no limit when we're talking dreams."

"Dreaming big is good," Laura said. "I hope you don't mind, but I ran into Sir Percy on my way here. I asked him to join us."

"Whatever for?"

"I hoped to share with him that map your father left. With your agreement, of course."

Amanda stiffened. "The man works for Hawkes."

"That's only what Hawkes believes. In truth, Percy is using Hawkes to further his own ends. I believe he could be a valuable ally."

"In what regard?"

Her words were punctuated by a loud rapping of knuckles against the front door.

Amanda rose, conscious of the documents, secured once more at her midsection. "I'm not sure about this. What do we really know about the man?"

"Very little, I'm afraid. But I do believe he could be useful in helping us discover whatever it is Hawkes is determined to keep hidden."

Amanda opened the door to see not Sir Percy standing before her, but Bradley Mason. She stared dumbfounded, mouth gaping open.

He doffed his hat. "Aren't you going to invite me in?"

"I was expecting someone else," she said rather churlishly, as she stepped aside to allow him entry.

"Percy's not far behind. I came to tell you I believe he is who he says he is. And that he can help us."

"Us?" Amanda asked, aware of Laura behind her nodding. "When did this become 'us'?"

"Trust me when I tell you there's a lot you don't know."

HAWKES STRODE through the empty house, his temper rising with every step he took. His time in jail awaiting trial had not improved his disposition one bit. The satisfaction of dumping the dead cat at the feet of the new Mrs. Brody Mason had only whetted his appetite for more of the same. And not just a dead animal.

"Isabela! Hernandez!" Not for the first time he wished he had a dog so he could kick it. What did a man have to do to get a little respect in his own home?

He pushed into the study. Jeffrey lounged behind his

desk, booted feet resting on the dusty wood surface, a glass of liquor in his hand.

"Save your voice," Jeffrey said, as Hawkes opened his mouth to let loose with another impatient bellow. "They're gone."

"Who's gone?" Hawkes thundered.

"The servants."

"What the hell—?"

"Their departure was no doubt hastened by the reality of likely never seeing the back wages they're owed, and your incredibly foul temper since you got out of jail."

"If those stupid greasers took a thing that didn't belong to them, I'll see them strung up."

Jeffrey emptied the contents of his glass in a single swallow. "One of these days you'll run into someone you can't bribe. Then what will you do?"

"What kind of nonsense are you talking, boy?" Hawkes made his way to the liquor cart, pushing Jeffrey's feet off his desk as he passed by. He poured himself a shot of bourbon. "'Stead of sitting around getting sloshed you should be out hiring new servants. Getting things set to rights. This place went to hell while I was away."

Jeffrey acted as if he hadn't even spoken. "I told Uncle Ian you'd get away with it. Killing my mother, that is."

"There you go again, talking nonsense about things you don't know nothing about."

"I figured out quite a few things while you were in jail."

Hawkes sneered at his son. "Bet that suited you. Playing lord of the manor. Getting too big for your britches."

"I know you played me for a fool. Sent me out west to bring Laura back here, pretending you didn't know who she was or the history between her and Brody." He rose and hitched his trousers. "You're going to have to find yourself another puppet. I'm done here with you and your manipulative ways."

Hawkes made a scoffing noise deep in the back of his throat. "You won't last five minutes in the real world without me wiping your ass."

They both turned toward the door at the sound of a carriage and driver pulling up out front. "Now what—?"

Jeffrey rose and picked up his hat, dusting it against his leg. "That'll be Uncle Ian."

Hawkes spat out his disgust. "That milksop brother of your ma's. Coming out here and having her body exhumed. Didn't know who he was dealing with, trying to pin a murder charge on Hawkes, did he? No, sir. He badly underestimated who and what I am."

"We all did."

Hawkes reached for a nearby rifle. "I'll happily run him off the property myself. Unless you got the stomach for it."

"Uncle Ian told me Mother's secret. That you're not my real father. Is that why you killed her?"

Hawkes raised the rifle and pointed it toward Jeffrey. "Get out!" he roared.

"I'm going," Jeffrey said. "Back to Boston. Back to my real family. I just stayed to tell you one thing. I'm glad you're not my real father. Glad it's not your tainted blood flowing through my veins."

The door slammed behind Jeffrey, and Hawkes slowly lowered his rifle. World was going to hell. But not until he finished what he'd set out to do. Rid the world of those miserable Masons, every last one of them. And tap into the richest vein of copper in the state.

All the while making sure the past stayed buried. Where it belonged.

BRADLEY'S GAZE shifted from Amanda to Laura and back to Amanda. The "us" question was a valid one. Unfortunately, he had no answer. At least not one that would satisfy them. "When something's not right, it affects everyone in Bullet," he muttered, saved by a loud knock at the door. "That'll be Sir Percy."

Amanda rose to get the door, and Laura went to fetch more tea cups for their guests.

"Ladies." Sir Percy doffed his hat and bowed in their direction. His gaze stalled on Bradley, and he straightened. "We meet again, Mr. Mason. In more favorable circumstances this time."

"No more danger of you trespassing now that you have Brody's okay for your search." He took the hand Percy offered. The man might play the dandy, but his hands were rough and calloused, obviously well acquainted with physical labor.

"Indeed," Percy said. "It's nice to have the blessing of the Mason brothers. And that of the lovely Mrs. Brody Mason." He made a big show of pressing a kiss to the back of Laura's hand. Bradley cleared his throat noisily, feeling unaccountably protective toward his new sister-in-law.

Next, Percy's bird-like eyes sought out Amanda. "And our lovely hostess. The lady with the map." Bradley scowled as Percy next captured Amanda's hand and kissed the back of it. Amanda pinkened becomingly.

Bradley decided to take charge. "You came to Bullet with stories of a buried ship filled with pearls."

"Not just any pearls. Most rare and valuable black pearls," Percy qualified, taking a seat at the table and accepting a cup of tea. Bradley looked around, wondering if

Amanda had anything stronger stashed than the bottle of brandy he'd fed to her the other evening.

Sir Percy was obviously a man after his own heart, for the good fellow pulled out a flask and splashed some amber liquid into his tea before he offered it to Bradley, who accepted gratefully.

"Does someone want to start at the beginning?" Bradley asked.

Amanda jumped in. "I might as well. I still don't know all, of course. Twenty some years back a lot of the stage-coaches coming in and out of Yuma were terrorized by a group of bandits known as 'Red's Rowdies' on account they always wore red bandannas hiding their faces." Her voice grew quiet. "I wasn't born yet. According to Ma, one day my pa never came home, and the gang was never seen nor heard from again."

"Someone killed them," Percy guessed.

"Ma always said nothing but a grave would keep my Pa away. He'd sworn this was his last job, and that by the time I arrived he'd be a regular family man. He left something with my ma to keep her safe."

Percy took a sip. "It must have worked. Here you are."

Bradley noticed the way Amanda twisted her hands in her lap. The telling wasn't easy for her, confessing to her father's criminal activity.

"Yup, just Ma and me all these years. Hawkes might have had other townsfolk quaking in their boots, but not Ma." Her voice lowered. "She was lonely though. One day I heard her talking to Pa like he was right here in this very room. Pretty soon after that her mind was gone. Wasn't safe to leave her alone; she could have wandered off or burned the place down. I told folks around here she was going on a trip and Doc Parsons arranged for her stay in a sanatorium near Yuma."

"Did you know what your father left with your mother to help keep you safe?"

"Not until recent. She seemed to brighten up for a short while near the end. Not long before she passed, she gave me an envelope, warning me to keep it someplace safe. She said she hoped I never needed to use it 'cause it could stir up quite a hornets' nest." She sighed. "Soon after, she was gone."

Percy looked to Laura. "And this map that almost got you killed, that was what Amanda received from her mother?"

Bradley noticed Laura's brief hesitation before she nodded. "Since you know so much about hunting down treasure and the like, I thought perhaps, with Amanda's approval, you could help figure out where the map might lead."

Percy crossed one leg over the other and studied his nails as if deep in thought. Bradley hoped he wasn't wrong about the man being deemed trustworthy. Above all, the newcomer was a treasure hunter. He didn't know much about the type, but safe to bet Percy was first, last and always out for himself.

"If the ladies agree to share the map with you, what's to stop you from absconding with whatever you find, leaving everyone here high and dry?"

Percy straightened. "Might I ask what your interest is in all this, my good man? I was under the impression you and your brothers have cattle to fatten up and drive west. No spare time to be dashing about with secret maps and the like."

"Miss Cooke is best friends with my sister-in-law. Naturally her well-being is of my concern. Someone broke in here and made off with a fake document. Once they figure that out, there's nothing to stop them from coming back a second time. Or a third."

"I see." Percy steepled his fingers together thoughtfully. "I take it you have some course of action in mind, to help keep her safe."

CHAPTER 3

Amanda felt the hated flush of embarrassment staining her cheeks. "I would appreciate it if you all didn't speak about me as if I was not here. I am more than capable of looking after myself. Been doing it my entire life."

Laura reached across the table and patted her hand. "No one doubts that for a second, Amanda. I certainly never expected to tangle with Hawkes the way I did. If he even thinks you know something that could compromise him, there's no saying what he might do."

Percy spoke up. "Your friend is right, my dear. You should not stay here alone."

Amanda glanced around the table. No reason to think anyone here had other than her best interests at heart, but she refused to give up the independent life she had created for herself. Even if it was lonely. She glanced over at Bradley. It was clear from today he considered her nothing but a liability. A burden. A helpless woman.

She rose and crossed the room. Reaching behind a pillow on the settee, she pulled out a pistol. "If whoever broke in here comes back, I am more than ready for them."

After making it clear she was not giving up the map to Percy or anyone else, two of her three visitors left. Laura first, followed by Percy. Amanda didn't miss the look Laura cast Bradley's way. A look that beseeched him to talk some sense into her.

Chin high, shoulders straight, she flashed him a defiant glare across the table. "It's quite obvious what you're doing. You and Laura have cooked up some scheme between you."

Bradley seemed suddenly very intent on the wood grain of the table between them. So she was right!

"Amanda, Laura and I both think you should come and stay on the ranch where you'll be safe."

She barked out a laugh of disbelief. "Since when is the ranch safe? Nothing stopped Hawkes from disrupting their wedding."

"That was mostly bluster. His way of letting us know he's fresh out of jail and we'd better look out. What happened here, that was different."

When she shook her head, he sighed and tried again. "For some reason the ranch is more personal to Hawkes. This gambit, trying to get his hands on your secret information, that's pure business. And nothing and no one gets in the way of Hawkes's business."

She crossed her arms on the table in front of her. "Don't think I don't appreciate your good intentions. I do. But I'm not moving to the ranch. Laura and Brody are newlyweds who need their time alone. Am I to move into the ranch house with you and your brothers? Before long the lot of you high-tail it off taking a herd of cattle west. What then, Bradley? And what of my work? I don't see myself travelling into town from the ranch and back at night."

He looked torn. As if part of him wanted her to agree to

stay at the ranch, while another part of him wished her miles away.

"You can have Brody's old room in the ranch house. We never all leave the ranch at the same time, so at least one or two of us will always be around. Besides, it would be handier for you to be at the ranch while Percy's helping us figure out the significance of that map your daddy left."

"I did not agree to share the map with Percy or anyone else."

Bradley rose, hat in hand. "Your friends care about you, Amanda. You're lucky in so many ways."

Amanda stood. Even at her full height Bradley towered nearly a foot above her, making her feel small and ... and what? Feminine? Weak? She refused to admit to herself that even now, here, she found his presence reassuring. He seemed so big and strong and invincible.

In spite of herself, she let out a soft sigh. "You're lucky too, you know with your big, rowdy, supportive family. It's quite different being an only child."

His scowl deepened. "At least you know who you are. Where you come from. I still have that mystery to unravel."

She caught her breath. She'd never given much thought to how it must feel to be an orphan. Yet despite how close-knit the Mason brothers were, it wasn't the same as blood. Let alone being left on the church steps as an infant. She felt an overwhelming swell of emotion threaten to choke her.

"Were you adopted shortly after birth?" she asked softly.

He gave his head a brusque shake. "Not till I was older." Right before her eyes, his gaze went to some deep, dark place of pain, and she sucked in her breath. She hadn't intended to cause him pain with his memories.

"How did you get to be so good with animals?"

"The circus."

She started to laugh, but seeing the serious look on his face, the laughter died in her throat.

Abruptly his face closed down as if he regretted telling her that much. "You should come stay at the ranch. The house ladies will get by without you for a while. Just until we have a few answers."

In spite of herself, she said, "I'll give it some thought."

Amanda checked the locks and windows half a dozen times before she turned in for the evening. Once in bed, she tossed and turned, alternately pulling up the coverlet then kicking it off, only slightly comforted by the loaded pistol under her pillow.

Old Mr. Adams, who sold it to her, had shown her how to load it. He'd even taken her out back of the store and set up a few empty tin cans for her to shoot at, just so she'd get used to the weight of it in her hand and the way her arm jerked when she fired.

She wasn't much of a shot. But if anyone got too close, she believed she could pull the trigger. Hopefully, it wouldn't ever come to that.

She was sipping her cup of tea in the morning, feeling far from refreshed, when she heard booted feet coming up the front steps. She jumped up and raced for her pistol, still beneath her pillow. A loud knock on the door echoed through the rooms and shook the windows.

"I'm coming. I'm coming," she called. It seemed unlikely robbers would be here in broad daylight knocking on the door, but to be sure she pulled back the lace curtain to see a familiar face.

"Good morning, Miss Cooke." Sir Percy swept into the house in his usual theatrical manner. "Sorry to disturb you this early, but I have an idea that simply won't wait to be discussed with you."

"Which is?" Amanda knew she sounded less than hospitable after her sleepless night.

"It occurs to me I require a base of operations here in town. Your house would be perfect!"

"You want to stay here? How unseemly." And yet the presence of another body, a male body at that, might allow her to sleep at night. What a shame she couldn't agree. Such a situation was bound to set tongues to wag and cause a minor scandal were she to have a man under her roof.

"Oh, no, no," Sir Percy tut-tutted. "I wish to rent the property for the duration of my time here in Bullet." He paced about as he spoke. "I need room to spread out my research documents. Plus, I am expecting the arrival any day now of a colleague to assist in the day-to-day details."

"I thought you were staying at the Hawkes ranch."

"Oh goodness, no." Sir Percy actually shuddered. "Never. I have been staying over the saloon. Most unsuitable digs, I might add."

He turned his attention back to matters at hand. "Seeing you have the offer of accommodation at the ranch, I would be more than happy to pay you for the kind rental of your home. Should anyone break in here and snoop about my papers ..." He laughed. "Allow me to say they will go hightailing off in the completely opposite direction. Red herrings are one of my many specialties."

Amanda pursed her lips, wondering if she was being played. Could this be something elaborately cooked up by Laura and Bradley? "I was under the impression treasure hunters stay out in the field, set up camp and the like."

"Some might. Afraid old Henny and I much prefer a bed to the cold hard ground. That will all change of course, once we pinpoint the site. Eventually we will end up roughing it, so to speak. But for now, the use of your home will suit us nicely."

Amanda heard a second knock at the door, softer this time.

"Oh, that'll be Henny now."

Amanda expected to see some grizzled-looking prospector-turned- treasure-hunter type on her porch. Instead, her breath was taken away by the stunning beauty of the woman before her. Her hair was black as a raven's wing and pulled straight back in a way that emphasized eyes the color of emeralds and high cheek bones that spoke to a foreign heritage.

Her voice, when she spoke, was melodious and faintly accented. "You must be Amanda. I'm Henrietta. Percy has told me so much about you."

HAWKES LOOKED round him in approval. High-backed leather wing chairs. Dark paneling and darker carpeting. Long velvet drapes drawn against the sunlight. Randall's fancy gentlemen's club was a place he could see himself joining.

A silent waiter delivered two heavy crystal glasses of scotch. Hawkes enjoyed seeing the faint ring his glass left on the highly polished wooden side table.

He raised his glass toward Randall, then drained it in a single gulp. "Nice digs," he said. "Most civilized." A few of the other members were scattered about the room, out of earshot. Most men were either reading a paper or napping.

"I thought we should meet someplace private, yet public at the same time," Randall said, rolling his scotch around in his glass before making a big deal out of holding it up to the dim pool of light cast by the lamp near his elbow. "Look at the legs on this," he said.

Hawkes harrumphed. Scotch with legs? Sounded obscene to him. He squinted at his empty glass and wondered how soon before a refill was on offer.

Randall moved on to stuffing his bulbous nose in the glass and sniffing loudly. "Amazing nose, wouldn't you agree?"

Now the whisky had both legs and a nose. Next thing Hawkes knew it would break into song. "Sure," he said.

By the time Randall actually took a sip of the damn stuff, Hawkes's patience was wearing thin. "Have you received the shipment?"

"Of course," Randall said, still fixated on the contents of his glass. "It's in my warehouse at the docks. I believe you'll be most pleased. They sent me some of that new gelatin dynamite. The latest thing, it's proven to be more water-resistant. Not to mention the latest style of electrical blasting caps. We're finding them really effective in our mines up north. Easy enough to set up a timing device if one knows what one is doing."

Hawkes sat forward in interest. "Do tell."

"We use a clock-type device to set the charge to detonate at a later time. Its invention has really cut down on the casualty rate among the mining crew."

Hawkes pursed his lips. He was far more interested in upping a particular casualty rate. But he didn't tell Randall that.

"I was surprised when I got your note saying you needed all this immediately. Last I heard, there's been several delays and you're still some time from setting up the copper mines."

"I believe in always being prepared," Hawkes said.

"Never quite know when circumstances can change with little or no warning."

BRADLEY AND BRODY rode the fence line in silence. The cattle had recently been moved to higher ground. The ability to move the herds west by rail had increased their operation capacity considerably. More head meant expanding their paddocks west and irrigating more ground.

Copper Moon Ranch was an unusual configuration by Arizona standards, with low-lying areas closer to the ranch house where the river widened, which made for easy irrigation and watering of cattle. To the east the land undulated into higher ground, some of which was mostly rock and sand, too barren to graze cattle or attempt to cultivate. The higher ground was where Laura had been accosted by Hawkes and almost killed. Bradley knew something on Amanda's map had sent Laura into that tangle of no-man's land, but whatever it was, Amanda wasn't sharing and Laura wasn't talking about it.

Brody broke the silence. "Laura's fair worried about her friend Amanda."

"I know." Bradley had wondered when the subject would be raised.

Brody gave him an assessing look. "Think there's any chance Amanda might change her mind and stay out here till things get resolved?"

Bradley blew out a breath. Why were the others acting, and him feeling, as if Amanda was his charge? Just because he'd been there the night of the break-in? "Someone ought to ask her."

Brody's look on him hardened, which was out of character. "I don't want anyone getting killed because of this situation with Hawkes."

Bradley nodded in agreement. "I hear tell Jeffrey high-tailed it out east with his uncle."

"Smart of him to get out from under Hawkes's thumb," Brody said. Almost losing Laura had spooked his friend, but rather than back off from Hawkes, the brothers only felt their resolution grow. "Hawkes'll always have his guns for hire."

Bradley cleared his throat and changed the subject. "Amanda believes her pa was once one of Hawkes's gang, back when the stagecoaches in and out of Yuma were getting robbed regular-like. If that's the case, it proves that even back then, Hawkes managed to skirt the law."

Brody nodded thoughtfully. Bradley knew they were both remembering the night when Joe, older brother to the twins, had been strung up right before their eyes. To this day, Hawkes still wore the homemade knife he'd taken from his victim like a badge of honor he enjoyed flaunting right before their eyes. Brody and Bradley exchanged a look, knowing all the brothers felt the same. Killing was too good for the likes of Hawkes. They wouldn't rest till Hawkes was first destroyed, piece by piece, then put into the ground.

Suddenly the sight ahead stabbed dread into his heart. "What the— " Bradley kicked his horse into a gallop and raced to where several head of cattle lay on their sides in an unnatural position. He leapt from his mount, Brody on his heels. Bradley knelt beside the steer and ran his hands over the hollowed-in flank. Most of the herd were still on their feet, many seeking out what little shade was available.

He looked up at Brody. "How long they been grazing here?"

"Had 'em moved about six days ago. Barron and Bishop oversaw the move. Nothing out of the ordinary."

Bradley squinted to where a fresh canal had been dug to bring in a water supply for the herd. "Anyone else have access?"

Brody shrugged. "It's hardly a fortress out here."

"Just remembering how Mrs. Hawkes was poisoned before she drowned."

"You think the cattle might have been poisoned?"

Bradley stood. "It's one possibility. Let's get the ones still on their feet moved to a different source of drinking water."

As Amanda listened to Henrietta and Percy's animated chatter about the latest findings in their quest for the ship of rare pearls, she had a feeling of being outnumbered and outmaneuvered, and realized she didn't mind as much as she would have thought. Not when it was clear others needed her home more than she did.

When Percy excused himself to return to his room above the saloon to retrieve some research papers, Amanda found herself alone with Henrietta and unaccountably tongue-tied. The other woman was so sophisticated and well-travelled, not to mention intelligent, that Amanda felt like a country bumpkin next to her.

"Percy says, you play the piano," Henrietta said. "My mother tried to have me learn, but I'm afraid I was all thumbs and totally tone-deaf, so eventually she gave up. I was the youngest of nine brothers, and a hopeless tomboy, much to her disappointment."

"Nine brothers," Amanda said, wide-eyed. "What was that like?"

Henrietta's laugh was like a beautiful musical note. "Frustrating for all of us. I never really fit in, and it was a relief to escape to London and live with Grandmama. Had I stayed behind I would have likely been miserable, saddled to someone as unsuitable as my father was for my mother. And every bit as unhappy."

"You help me realize that maybe being an only child wasn't so bad after all."

Henrietta gave her hand a friendly squeeze. "Believe me, I felt like an only child in a family of twelve. I never fit in."

Amanda had been eyeing Henrietta's clothing, envying her the freedom of movement in what appeared to be a cross between a riding skirt and men's trousers. "Is that the latest style in Europe? What you're wearing."

"What, this?" Henrietta laughed. "Mercy, no. I'm sure the great fashion houses of Europe would be appalled. I had this specially tailored at a mens' wear shop in Boston when I came to America. The crazy places I get dragged along to with Percy, women's fashions just aren't suitable." She laughed again. "Think there's any chance it'll catch on out here?"

Amanda flushed and wondered how it would feel to have such confidence in one's decisions. To wear whatever she felt like and go wherever she pleased and not care a fig what anyone else thought.

BRADLEY AND BRODY parted ways in the stables after seeing to their horses. Bradley felt an uncomfortable twinge of emotion as he watched the other man make his way to his cozy new home and waiting bride.

Funny the way Brody getting hitched had changed

things up around the place. For as long as Bradley could recall, it had been a united front of brotherhood, one for all and all for one. Now Laura lived here with Brody, and thoughts of Amanda unsettled his mind at the most inconvenient of times.

No wonder a woman on a ship was considered bad luck. He wondered if you could say the same thing about a ranch. Not that he didn't like Laura. Quite the opposite. He was happy for Brody that he and Laura moved past everything that had happened ten years ago into a bright, new future. A future that would be much rosier once Hawkes had been dealt with once and for all.

He'd managed to push Amanda from his thoughts while they were dealing with the sick cattle, but now, with that behind him, she crept right back in like she belonged there. Or never left.

He pushed open the door to the sprawling ranch house where he lived with the other brothers and stopped short, jaw slack at the sight that greeted him. Amanda stood at the stove stirring something in a black-bottom pot, wearing the cutest apron with ruffles accenting her curves while escaped wisps of fiery red hair curled around her face. The twins hovered nearby, hanging on her every word. No one saw him enter, so he slammed the door hard behind him. Three pairs of eyes turned his way.

One side of Amanda's mouth quirked upward in an engaging half-smile. "The twins and I are having a chili cook-off. Theirs against mine. Loser cleans up."

Bradley moved to the sink, plucked up a glass and pumped himself a measure of water, which he stared at suspiciously. If the cattle's water source had been poisoned, were any of them safe?

He turned and glowered at Bishop and Barron. "Could

have used your help today. Had to turn the cattle back to a different paddock. Something's wrong with the water where they were. At least I hope it's the water."

"Brody said not to leave the homestead unattended." Bradley thought it was Bishop who answered him. The twins were identical and hard to tell apart, but Bishop tended to talk slower and take things a little more seriously.

Bradley addressed Amanda. "You here for dinner or come to your senses and staying a while?"

Amanda flushed in that adorable way that she had. "Turns out Sir Percy needed a home base for himself and his helper. It would have been rude to refuse. And since you and Laura had been so adamant about me being safer here ..." Her voice trailed off. "I hope it's all right that I'm here. The twins showed me to Brody's old room."

"It's fine." Bradley grabbed a towel off the back of the door and headed outside to get cleaned up before he ate. He didn't want Amanda noticing he smelled like the cattle he'd been tangling with most of the day.

"Don't Laura and Brody eat with us?" Amanda felt strangely awkward seated at the table, the lone female between the three brothers. As an only child, dinners had been somber affairs and, as Ma's mind slowly slipped away, they became downright depressing. Once Ma was in the sanatorium, she had accepted her lonely meal times.

This evening proved anything but, with the conversation bouncing from the possibly poisoned cattle to Hawkes being on the loose again to the new herd coming their way from Mexico.

"We don't see the newlyweds at meals much these days,"

Barron, at least she thought it was Barron, answered. The conversation was so loud and boisterous, she couldn't keep up as the brothers raised their voices to be heard above the others. That is, when they weren't good-naturedly interrupting one other.

"Wonder if this is the trip where Braydon brings back a little señorita from down south," Bishop said.

Bradley spoke up. "He does have a soft spot for the ladies."

"Nah," Barron said. "They got a soft spot for him." He turned to Amanda. "Braydon grew up in a 'fancy house' in Yuma. Never knew which one of the ladies was his Ma, but he surely did get an education into the fairer sex, if you cotton my meaning."

"Barron." Bradley spoke in a low, warning voice. "That's hardly dinner time conversation. Especially with a lady in our midst."

Barron cocked his head. "Begging pardon, Amanda. House of bachelors, we get used to speaking what's on our mind. This is mighty delicious chili you made. I think you might have Bishop and I beat."

"Secret ingredient," Amanda said, smiling into her bowl. "A little pinch of chocolate."

She was interrupted by a loud clattering on the front porch. The door flew open to let in the rest of her new roommates, back from the cattle drive, dirty, stinky, and hungry.

As the chili was inhaled, the room grew noisier by the second, and Amanda thrived on every second of it. Afterward, the twins good-naturedly cleaned the dishes while the newcomers took themselves down to the river for a much-needed bath. Which left her and Bradley alone in the sitting room.

"You're sure you don't mind that I'm here?" Amanda asked as the silence stretched tautly between them.

From his seat on the settee, Bradley had been staring off into space, and jerked toward her as she spoke, almost as if he'd forgotten she was there. "Sorry," he said gruffly. "I was someplace else. Need to figure what's what with the water. Can't afford to lose half a herd."

"Is it possible for someone to poison just one section of the canal near shore?"

"It would take a whole lot of arsenic, and that's for sure. A few of the herd are poorly. If they don't recover, we should have our answer. Evidence of arsenic will show up in the organs."

"Like it did with poor Mrs. Hawkes."

"For all the good it did."

They were both silent for a moment, thinking of the man who had been accused and acquitted of killing his wife. The man who more than likely killed Amanda's father along with the rest of the gang members before she was born.

"He does get away with murder," Amanda said with a sigh.

"Don't we know it," Bradley said darkly. "Saw him kill the twins' older brother with our own eyes. All of us witnessed it, too late to stop it."

Amanda sucked in her breath. "Oh, Bradley. How dreadful for you. No wonder you all hate him." Unable to stop help herself, she was on her feet and by his side in seconds.

His eyes were dark and unreadable. "We swore an oath in blood to take him down. Slow and painful-like. Piece by piece."

She sat next to him and rested her hand on his forearm where he'd rolled up the sleeve of his cotton shirt. His skin was warm and darkened from the sun, liberally sprinkled with dark hair. She heard his breath catch, saw him glance down at her lightly freckled hand atop his arm.

He took her hand but rather than brush it off his arm, turned it over and raised it to his lips. Her world went still as he traced a moist, damp circle in the middle of her palm. Flutters in her throat trickled down to her stomach and beyond. His coal-black eyes met hers, alight with purpose.

He moved slowly, giving her lots of time to draw back. Ran the back of his hand gently down the side of her face before he cupped his other hand around the back of her neck. Every nerve ending in her body leapt to life like tiny lightning bolts, sparking beneath his touch. Then he angled her head the way he wanted it before he took his mouth with hers.

She felt the warmth of his breath on her lips seconds before he claimed her. Branded her with his hot, hungry need.

CHAPTER 4

H is mouth played with hers as if they were old friends. Teasing sips and nibbles were followed by deep penetration and ownership. Amanda gave herself over to the myriad of sensations, sighing deeply into him. How often had she longed for this? Dreamt of this?

Dreams that proved nothing compared with the reality of being caught tight against Bradley, willing captive to his possession. Beneath her chemise, her bosom tightened into reactive pleasure buds. She grew overly aware of the brush of her underpinnings sending heat waves of need into her womanly chamber. What might it feel like if it was Bradley's hand there? Or his mouth?

She whimpered and shifted closer, needing more, disappointed as he slowly withdrew. His hands gentled, along with his lips, until there was air between them. Air fraught with tension. With unfinished business.

He ran a hand through his tousled, dark hair. "I'm sorry," he said gruffly, pulling back and getting to his feet. "It won't happen again. I don't want you to feel trapped here, afraid every time you see me I'll be pushing up against you like some rutting goat."

Amanda blinked up at him, her vision still hazed by the aftermath of his kiss. She raised a hand to her lips, which felt puffed and tingly. She rose also. Was this the pattern they were destined to repeat over and over? Get the least bit close, then retreat to their respective safe places?

She was proud of the decorum with which she held herself, as if nothing had happened. As if he had not just rocked her world with a single kiss. "Goodnight, Bradley."

Damn it!

He had no business giving in to the temptation to kiss her.

Now things were bound to be hell-and-high-water awkward as long as she stayed on the ranch. Drat Laura and her bright ideas! Not to say he hadn't been worried about Amanda after the break-in at her home. But he didn't need her underfoot all the time. Maybe he could suggest to Brody and Laura that Amanda stay over with them.

Braydon sauntered into the parlor looking as carefree and confident as ever. Bradley envied the other man that air of confidence. Growing up in a house of ill repute meant Braydon wasn't getting walloped with a leather belt every time he opened his eyes or his mouth. He shuttled that thought into the past where it belonged.

"How's the new herd?" Bradley asked.

"Hungry. The twins tell me you and Brody had to move the others today."

"Yup. Too early to tell what was making them sick, but lucky we caught it when we did."

Braydon nodded. "Saw our little houseguest scurry up the steps looking a tad disheveled. Anything go on in here that oughtn't to?"

Bradley rose and went to push past him. "Nothing to do with you."

Braydon stopped him with an arm blocking the doorway. "You don't need me to tell you there's women and then there's women. That little gal is not the trifling type. Lots of the other kind where I come from."

"You're not telling me anything I don't know."

"I've seen the way she looks at you with those big green eyes when she thinks no one is watching. She's under our roof. Our protection. That means she stays safe. Gentleman's code of honor."

Bradley snorted. "Since when has anyone accused you of being a gentleman?"

Braydon responded with a smug smile. "I have my moments."

Bradley headed upstairs to bed, Braydon's words ringing in his ears. Shoot if his big brother wasn't right as usual. He needed to put things to rights, friendship only, between him and Amanda. Treat her like a little sister. So why did he have such a hard time falling asleep, knowing she was in the bedroom right next door, nothing but a thin wooden wall between them?

Bradley woke up early, listening for sounds of Amanda stirring. He managed to time it perfectly, running into her on the way downstairs. "Fancy a trip into Yuma today?"

She slanted him a look that could only be termed suspicious. He forced a smile that he hoped looked nonchalant. "We can stop by your house if you like. See how Percy is settling in. Make sure everything is okay."

She tilted her head, considering. "Why do I feel like

there's something suspect behind your offer? Does someone here want me out of the way?"

Now he'd done it! She was afraid to be alone with him. "No catch. Just thought you might like to get off the ranch. Take your mind off things for a bit."

She took her time with her answer. "In that case I'll change into riding clothes."

"I'll grab a bite and see to the horses. Meet you in the barn."

SHE WOULD NEVER UNDERSTAND MEN! After that one toe-curling, soul-rendering kiss, Bradley had leapt away from her as if burned. But how could she be expected to understand men, having grown up with no father or brothers? Bradley had to feel the same about women, having no mother or sisters, eventually winding up here on this ranch with all men.

Amanda felt a flicker of pity for her friend, Laura. But not too much pity. Laura was at least married to the love of her life. She had a home and a husband. Even if she had to put up with this motley lot of set-in-their-ways bachelors.

Once they were under way, Bradley rode slightly ahead of her, one hand on his rifle as he scanned the roadway ahead as if half-anticipating an ambush, but they passed Hawkes's sprawling ranch without incident.

She nudged her mount into a canter and caught up to him. "You're not expecting any trouble, are you?"

He nudged his Stetson back with a knuckled fist. "Never hurts to be on guard."

"What's in Yuma?' she asked.

"Veterinarian I know. He's friends with a man who's a

brilliant chemist. I'm hoping that between the two of them, they can analyze the water that made the steers sick. It'll help some if we know what we're up against."

If anything, Bradley looked more serious than usual as he spoke. Amanda figured there had to be a lot he wasn't telling her. "Are you worried about the ranch house water supply as well?"

"Like I said, never hurts to be on guard."

Which didn't tell her a darn thing.

They made the rest of the trip in silence, Amanda taking her cues from Bradley, eyes probing the shadowy country-side, one hand never far from her pistol. Once they reached the outskirts of Yuma, she saw Bradley visibly relax, and she did as well. It had been a long time since she had ventured this far from Bullet, and it was exciting to be not only here, but here with Bradley.

Music blared forth from a new-looking two-story wooden structure that hadn't been here on her last trip. "What's that place?"

"New music hall," Bradley said. "Opened up last year."

"What do they do there?"

"The kind of entertainment that isn't found in a saloon, I guess. I've heard they perform musical plays, have dances, teach music lessons, and host socials for all ages. In a town this size, the dances are a way for men and women to meet each other."

"What a brilliant idea. And all under one roof." The only respectable place in Bullet to meet anyone of the opposite sex was at church. Amanda was always too busy playing the piano to even notice if there were any interesting men in the congregation. No wonder she was fixing on being an old maid. "We could use something like that in Bullet."

"No doubt it would liven up the place. But there's always

folks who don't want things livened up. People who like things just the way they are."

"No one likes the way things are, what with Hawkes terrorizing honest working folk and running them off their land," Amanda said, primly.

"He'll get his one of these days," Bradley said darkly.

"From your lips to God's ears," she said.

When Bradley dismounted in front of the veterinarian's office, Amanda followed suit. Being here in Bradley's company, she could almost imagine they were on a date.

Bradley introduced her to Monarch as his neighbor, so the vet assumed she, too, had a vested interest in the results of the water samples Bradley had brought with him.

"Leave these with me a few hours. If I don't get anything concrete, I'll head over to Mervin's," Monarch said.

"Appreciate that," Bradley said, looking around the outer office. "Busy these days?"

"Too busy," the vet said. "Don't forget, anytime you want a job, you got one here."

"Kinda like where I'm at right now, but you never know."

"Just keep it in mind."

"We'll run a few errands," Bradley said. "Be back in a couple hours. The horses okay where they are?"

"They'll be fine. You two run along and have some fun," the vet said, with a look that caused Amanda to blush to the roots of her hair.

"What did he mean by that?" she asked Bradley, once they were standing on the wooden sidewalk out front.

Bradley shrugged. "Beats me. Let's go over to the café and grab a bite."

Amanda reached out and caught his arm before she even realized what she was doing. "After that, if there's time, can we go take a look at the music hall?"

Bradley gave her a searching look. "Why the sudden interest?"

She wasn't about to tell him the truth. How her conversation with Laura had got her thinking about dreams and her future. "I play the piano. I'd like to see how it's set up. How it operates."

"Thinking of quitting your night job and moving here to Yuma?"

"Anything is possible. I know Bullet's my home and all, but somedays there doesn't seem to be much of a future there for a single gal." She gave a weighted sigh. "Meeting Henrietta the other day, hearing about some of her adventures in other parts of the world, surely did give me something to think about."

"I wouldn't set too much store in that. Strikes me as she's probably just as lonely as the rest of us."

Amanda stopped in her tracks and faced him. "I wouldn't have thought I'd ever hear you say you were lonely. Not living with all the brothers at the ranch."

His eyes found hers with an intimate look that rocked her to the soles of her feet. "Ever feel lonely even though you're in the midst of a crowd?"

He knew!

Amanda pressed her palm to her suddenly racing heart. "All the time."

The café wasn't busy as it was between the breakfast hour and the noon time meal. Amanda had just decided that she would order a pot of tea when Bradley surprised her by ordering vanilla ice cream for them both.

"Can't get this in Bullet," he said, as the fancy glass dishes were delivered to the table, each with a generous scoop of the beginning-to-melt-delicacy.

"I've heard of ice cream but never tried it," Amanda admitted.

"Now that," Bradley said, "is all wrong."

Amanda took her cue from Bradley, picked up her spoon and divided off a small mouth-size portion. The metal of the spoon was cold against her tongue, its contents cool, creamy and sweet with a hint of vanilla. Her eyes widened in shock at the sensation.

Across from her, Bradley stopped wolfing his down like a starving man, and gave her a genuine smile that sent butterflies to her tummy. "Good?"

"Fantastic," she said, swirling her tongue slowly through the second bite and the third, feeling the delicious concoction melt against her tongue and slide down her throat.

Bradley finished his and sat back, arms crossed over his chest, watching her with a pleased expression. She put down her spoon feeling unaccountably shy. "I don't think I can eat with you watching me like that."

"What?" he said. "I'm merely enjoying your pleasure at experiencing something new."

Amanda felt her heart swell. Everything she did with Bradley seemed to result in new, previously unexperienced pleasure. Abruptly he reached across the table toward her, ran his finger over her lower lip, then showed her the glop of ice cream he had rescued before he popped his finger into his mouth. Amanda just smiled into her dish and proceeded to take smaller bites, careful not to get the treat all over her face.

After their ice cream, Bradley indulged her further by heading for the music hall. Amanda's tingle of anticipation dulled to disappointment at seeing the front door firmly locked. She stood on tiptoe to try to peer through the window, but the glass panes had been painted black. Probably to stop anyone from doing that very thing.

"That's that," she said, stepping back with a sigh. "I appreciate you trying."

"Not so fast," Bradley said. He took her arm, which caused an entirely different tingle, and steered her around the side of the building to the back. Sure enough, the rear door stood ajar, propped open against a rock that prevented it from closing.

"Come on." He pulled it open all the way and stepped to one side, gesturing for her to precede him.

"Do you think we should?"

"Ever do anything you're unsure about? Take a chance?"

Other than kissing him?

"Not normally," she said.

His dark eyes bored into hers and a rush of heat snaked its way up her spine. "I don't believe you."

She blinked in surprise. No one ever challenged the church pianist. They all took her at her word. With a loud sniff she marched past him, head high, shoulders back.

The first two doors they passed were closed and lettered "fillies" and "stallions". Changing rooms, Amanda guessed.

From there, the corridor opened into a massive hall with a stage at one end. Half a dozen dancers were up on stage, engrossed in what looked to be practice steps. No one paid her and Bradley the slightest mind. Together, they hugged the shadows at the back of the room, staying mostly out of sight. Amanda felt a crazy excitement stir as she tried to imagine the hall at night. Alive with lantern light, music, moving bodies.

"Have you ever been here at night?" she whispered.

"No. But I'll bring you some night if you want. Provided you tell me what's sparking the sudden interest."

She cocked him a look. Had he just offered to bring her here to the music hall one night? Another new experience?

Her guard rose. No doubt he found her naivete and lack of worldliness amusing. Henrietta would no doubt have eaten ice cream dozens of times and visited music halls all around the world.

"Just an idea. Something Laura and I were talking about."

He fell silent at that and mercifully didn't press her for more information. Truthfully, she didn't even know what she might say. Her brain was awhirl with half-formed thoughts and ideas. None of which she was ready to share.

She liked that he didn't feel inclined to chat but left her in silence to her observations. She glanced over at him, wondering if he was bored.

His smile was impossible to read. "Seen your fill?"

In truth, she could have stayed there all day, soaking up the action and atmosphere, so unlike anything in her world, but Bradley had clearly seen enough. "Yes, thank you."

They left the same way they came in, through the back without anyone noticing them, and headed to the vet's office. Monarch took them into his private office and closed the door so they couldn't be overheard. He took off his spectacles and pinched the bridge of his nose. He looked either tired, or troubled. Amanda couldn't tell which.

"I gather you found something in the water sample I left. What is it?" Bradley asked impatiently.

"You're right and you're wrong," the vet said. "Your cattle have been poisoned. But not with arsenic. The sample you brought in contains vast amounts of salt."

He imparted further bad news in that the worst-affected cattle were unlikely to recover. He offered to come out and examine the deceased members of the herd, but there seemed to be little doubt in his mind about his findings.

All too soon, it seemed, her day in Yuma with Bradley was wrapping up.Amanda kept sneaking sideways glances at him on the ride back. He must have a lot on his mind, so she kept quiet as well. As they approached Bullet, Bradley pulled up and slowed till she was within earshot. "Fancy stopping by your place? I'd like a word with Percy, if he's there."

"Fine with me." Amanda wondered why he was seeking out Sir Percy, but guessed she would find out soon enough.

When no one answered the door, Bradley scribbled a brief note, which he folded over and handed to Amanda. "Can you leave this inside where Percy is likely to find it? It's important."

"Of course." She dug out her door key and did his bidding before they mounted up and headed back to the ranch.

Their arrival signaled the end of her day with Bradley. The entire day had felt so special. From the ice cream to the dance hall to being with Bradley when he received the findings from the vet. Was it wrong of her to long for more?

Or was this where he did his usual disappearing and silent act toward her? If only she was witty and glamorous like Henrietta, capable of sparking Bradley's interest so he saw her as a woman.

As they neared the house, Bradley's mount bypassed the barn and headed toward the river, Amanda's horse following suit. To her surprise the horses didn't stop at the water's edge for a drink. Instead, they galloped straight in, splashing water everywhere. In seconds Amanda was soaked yet exhilarated at the cooling sensation after their long ride.

Bradley dismounted and cupped a handful of water, which he raised to his lips and drank.

Amanda remained mounted. "Any traces of salt?"

"Tastes fine," Bradley said. The thirsty horses each took a long drink before Bradley led them out and off to one side near a clump of sweet grass.

Amanda dismounted and tugged off her hat before she ran a hand through her perspiration-dampened hair, releasing it from its loose braid. Her riding skirt was stuck to her damp skin. Impulsively she pulled off her wet riding boots, peeled off her stockings, hitched up her skirt and stepped into the cool water.

She glanced up in time to see Bradley join her with an approving smile that warmed her insides and made her bosom feel fuller. Perhaps he did see her as a woman after all. She giggled as he hopped from foot to foot while he struggled to pull off his own boots.

"Last one in is a rotten egg."

Amanda laughed. "What does that even mean?"

"Don't ask me. Something I heard the other day. Made me think of Hawkes. Turn around."

She turned to face the shore. Something whizzed over her head as, piece by piece, Bradley's discarded clothing landed in a heap near the horses. Which had to mean he was—

In spite of herself, she blushed.

"Coming in?" A short distance away he splashed, waist-deep. Droplets of water glistened on his bronze skin. His chest was liberally sprinkled with dark hair that arrowed below the waterline. He ducked his head below the surface, then came up, tossing back wet dark hair until it slicked tight to his skull. "I dare you."

Cool water lapped at her ankles, and it wasn't hard to

imagine it sluicing over her body, cooling her overheated flesh. Far too tempting a dare to turn down. She waded to shore where she divested herself of her riding skirt and jacket, retaining her cotton eyelet chemise and bloomers for modesty's sake.

The water was bracing cold as she inched her way in, past her ankles to her knees, then higher. She stood on tiptoe, sucking in her breath as cold water swirled near her female parts. She knew without looking down that her nipples had hardened into tight nubs.

She squealed when she was hit by a spray of cold water, courtesy of Bradley, who stood laughing at her. She retaliated with a robust splash of her own and got him in the face.

"Why you—!"

Before she could guess his intentions, he caught her around the waist and lifted her clean off her feet. As he swung her in a wide arc, the sunlight turned to rainbows in the spray.

All too soon, he set her down. His hands lingered, ever so briefly, on her waist before he released her. Slightly dizzy, she tottered a little before her feet found purchase on the silty river bottom.

Bradley caught her arms to help steady her. She opened her mouth to thank him, but the words snagged in her throat. All form of speech, all coherent thought, fled from her brain at the intense look as his dark eyes caught and held hers.

Their surroundings grew still. All she could hear was the overloud pounding of her own heart. Impulsively she laid her hands flat on his chest, thrilling at the feel of water-cooled male flesh and the ridges of well-defined muscles. Beneath her palm, his heart raced in tandem with hers.

His eyes grew heavy with intent as he pulled her closer.

Her hands naturally migrated to the indentation of his lean waist as her bosom brushed the hard wall of his chest. Heat shot through her, from her bosom to her womanly parts and beyond, a heavy warmth that rippled through her veins like thick honey.

She tilted her head and slowly dampened her lips, ready for his kiss. Her lips pouted with need before being crushed beneath his. He kissed her as if his very survival depended on this. On her.

She breathed into him, took from him and breathed again, lightheaded within the embrace. The feel of his skin beneath her hands. His bare chest plastered against her wet underthings. Rather than a barrier, her clothing was an enticement, pebbling her skin with goosebumps of excitement and desire.

His lips moved from hers to the hollow between shoulder and neck, and fresh longing swamped her. Her body felt boneless. Pliant. She swayed against him, afraid her legs would no longer hold her.

"Bradley! What the—"

Dazed, she looked up to realize they were no longer alone. Slowly the two of them drew apart and turned to face Brody and Laura, closely followed by Sir Percy and Henrietta. Amanda gulped a huge swallow.

Laura's eyes were wide with disbelief. Amanda opened her mouth to try and explain, then closed it abruptly. She knew frolicking with Bradley wasn't seemly. She had so longed for his kisses. But not at the sacrifice of everyone's good opinion. Her heart grew heavy, knowing she had let her friend down.

Wordlessly, Brody dismounted while Percy and Henrietta appeared very engrossed with staring over their heads into the distance. Brody's disapproving look toward Bradley was punctuated by the flight of Bradley's shirt and trousers through the air to land in the water near where Bradley stood.

"Laura," Brody said. "Can you please take everyone up to the house? I need to have a word alone with Bradley."

CHAPTER 5

Hawkes tapped his pen against the thick assayer's report that recently landed on his desk. Across from him sat Don Lucas and the assayer the Mexican had hired.

"I told you there would be copper," Don Lucas said.

Hawkes longed to wipe the smug look off the greaser's face. Not for one second was he willing to admit that the report contained a string of long words that he hadn't a clue what they meant.

He sat back in his chair as if holding court, rolling his pen between his fingers. "I already knew there was copper. But neither of us was sure exactly where on the ranch the vein would be. Or if it would be just copper ore."

"My findings indicate it to be of the purist quality," the assayer said hastily.

"The first deposits will be relatively easy to access," Don Lucas said. "Might I remind you the clock is ticking on the investment made by myself and my partners?"

Hawkes grunted. He no longer had the funds which had been advanced to him. A few sour investments had seen to that. Which meant he needed to play for time.

Don Lucas continued. "You assured me it was a simple matter before I saw your name on the deed to the ranch, the claim staked, and the work under way."

"Yeah, well. I'm the one dealing with those Masons. They can be a slippery lot."

With an impatient noise, Don Lucas stood. "You assured me you had things handled. I took you at your word."

"We shook on it, didn't we?" Hawkes said.

"Handshake or no handshake, I hear rumors that your word is not always your bond."

Hawkes sputtered with anger. How dare this stupid greaser question him? "My word is good. I'll tear apart any liar who says anything different."

Lucas's forefinger tapped the gold watch strapped to one wrist. "Tick, tock."

BRADLEY WADED to shore and managed to struggle his way into his wet pants and stab his arms into his shirt sleeves, not bothering with the buttons. Only a few times before had he been on the receiving end of Brody's wrath, and from the look of things here today, he expected this time to be a doozy.

Usually Brody was pretty easy-going with a relatively slow fuse, but give a reason to ignite that fuse and watch out. The oldest of all of them by at least a few years, Brody had never fully shed his big-brother mentality and acted like the others still needed his guidance and protection.

When he couldn't stand the silence any longer, he spoke up. "I know what you're thinking, but it's not the way it looks."

He flinched from the cold, brittle anger that emanated

from every pore of Brody's being. "You have no idea what I'm thinking."

Bradley tried to defuse things. "It was totally innocent. Brother-sister horseplay."

"I've never seen anyone lip-locked with his sister." Brody crossed his arms over his chest. "Amanda is not only my wife's best friend, she's here under our protection. You have compromised her reputation. And not just in front of Laura and I."

Bradley narrowed his gaze. "What are you trying to say?"

"I expect you to do the honorable thing."

Bradley stopped what he was doing, trying to get into his boots, and turned. "The honorable thing?"

"Congratulations!" Brody said dryly. "Consider yourself betrothed."

"Brody. Wait! You can't mean—" He spread his hands flat. "Hell, man. Nothing happened."

"That's not the way things appeared to everyone else. Amanda's reputation is on the line. This has to be contained and fast."

"I can't marry her. I'm not even husband material."

Brody cocked him a long, telling look. "You should have thought of that before you took your pants off." He turned and rode toward the ranch house. Slowly Bradley unclenched his fists, aware there was nothing to rail against except himself and his own impulsive stupidity.

He looked toward the river. What he ought to do is march right in there and drown himself. He was no good to anyone. His own mother gave him away. He wasn't worth saving. He wasn't worth loving.

His thoughts landed on Amanda. Odds were, she didn't want to get married any more than he did. They were both orphans, likely feeling somewhat abandoned. A bit lost.

Surely, they could work their way through the madness into the light.

When he thought about Hawkes sending someone in to trash her home, his blood boiled. She was the innocent one in all this. Brody was right. It was up to him to make sure she was safe.

Maybe a promise of marriage would achieve that. They could wait things out until Hawkes was stifled once and for all, then release each other from any sort of commitment. One day they might even look back and laugh about this.

He took one last look toward the river, but he'd never been one to take the coward's way out. Rather than rush back to the ranch house, he began rehearsing in his mind exactly what he might say.

AMANDA QUICKLY WENT in search of dry clothing, still not understanding all the hullabaloo about her having a swim with Bradley. There was nothing more to it than their day in Yuma. Or their time at the music hall.

Excitement made her movements clumsy as she changed and then joined the others downstairs. She couldn't wait to speak with Laura to share her dreams and her plans. Which, unfortunately, would have to wait until there were fewer people around.

Sir Percy was all but bouncing off the walls as he waited for Bradley. She had no idea what had been in the note Bradley had left, but it seemed enough to send the treasure hunter into another realm. From across the room, Henrietta watched him indulgently. Obviously, she was accustomed to seeing him like this. She also noticed Henrietta and Braydon sneaking furtive glances at each other when they each thought the other wasn't looking.

Before she could ponder that more, Brody was back. She glanced over his shoulder as he joined them, but there was no sign of Bradley. She swallowed thickly. Surely the two of them had not had an altercation on her part. Land sakes. The last thing she wanted to do was drive a wedge between the brothers. Perhaps she ought not to have come to stay here.

Across the room, Laura was bustling around making coffee and ensuring everyone was seen to, the perfect rancher's wife, Amanda thought admiringly. How did her friend intuitively know what to do?

Just then Laura pulled her aside, out of earshot of the others. "Brody said you should wait out on the porch for Bradley."

Amanda did as she was bid, waited outside on the porch, to no avail. She had no idea how much time had passed before she gave up and went back inside. Laura must have gotten things wrong.

Before she could question her further, Amanda heard a thud and turned to see the door swing open to reveal a damp and disheveled Bradley. As if on cue, the room fell silent. All eyes were on Bradley as he raised his chin a notch and let his eyes pass over each individual person gathered, one at a time.

His brothers. Laura. Percy and Henrietta. Finally, his gaze found her and she felt her insides flutter. What was going on? Why had she been told to wait outside for him?

He cleared his throat. "I have news," he said finally. "Took a water sample in to Yuma today. Yes, the cattle were poisoned. But not how we thought. It was salt toxicity, which apparently happens more often than is diagnosed. We can consider ourselves lucky we only lost a few head."

"I say, that is marvelous good news," Sir Percy enthused. "I knew it as soon as I read your note about the salt."

"Not if they were your cattle," Braydon groused.

"But don't you see," Percy continued. "It means Henny and I are totally on the right track about the salt marshes. Over time the salt marshes evaporated and left the pearl ship stranded. Eventually the ship was buried in the sand, exactly as I surmised." As he spoke, he rubbed his hands together with glee.

"It's exciting," Henrietta concurred. "All that painstaking research paying off."

"I have other news," Bradley said gruffly, before they all started talking about the treasure. Once again all eyes turned his way. "Amanda and I are getting hitched."

Amanda felt her world spin and go black.

BRADLEY JUMPED FORWARD and caught her before she hit the ground. He tried to make a joke. "First time I've ever sent a woman into a swoon so she fell at my feet." No one even cracked a smile. He tried again. "Anyone got any smelling salts?"

In his arms, Amanda lay limp and white. Laura rose. "Take her upstairs. I'll sit with her."

She didn't have to tell Bradley twice. He was all too happy to unburden himself, not just physically, but emotionally.

In the bedroom he laid Amanda down and watched as Laura hastily loosened her top button. He rocked back on his heels and shoved his hands in his pockets feeling more useless than ever. "Guess she doesn't want to marry me."

Laura gave him a hard look. "Did you ever think maybe she'd prefer to be asked? Not told in front a roomful of people."

"Brody didn't give me any choice."

Laura placed her hands on her hips. "Bradley Mason, there is a right way and a wrong way to do things. Time you figured out the difference." Amanda stirred, and Laura hastened to her side. "You'd best get out of here in case she opens her eyes and faints right away again at the sight of you."

Bradley was only too happy to make his escape. He heard the animated chatter of the family and their guests downstairs. Rather than join in, he ducked out the back door. It was setting up to be a clear night, the slowly darkening sky already scattered with a handful of stars. As usual, he'd made a mess of everything! For the first time in his life, he'd started to feel a sense of belonging, being a bona fide part of a community, and it was all blowing up around him.

Slowly he made his way to the barn to check on the animals. Seemed like that was all he was good for these days.

AMANDA SLOWLY OPENED her eyes and got her bearings. As she focused on the familiar, faded wallpaper, she realized she was on the ranch, in the room where she was staying. Laura sat next to the bed.

"What happened?" Her mouth and lips were dry, her words barely intelligible, even to her.

Laura smiled. "You fainted is all."

Amanda pushed herself up. "I don't faint."

"Apparently you do when you get a clumsy proposal."

Amanda flopped back down onto the pillow. Everything came rushing back. Her day with Bradley. His blunt statement to the group downstairs. "That was hardly a proposal. More like a joke. Why did Bradley say such a ridiculous thing? We're not getting married."

Laura smoothed Amanda's hair back from her face with a gentle hand. "Whether you do or you don't, it would be good if Hawkes believes you are under the protection of Bradley and all the others here."

"Isn't my staying here enough?"

"Brody is worried for your reputation. Bradley agreed." She smiled again. "I don't know about you, but I've always wanted a sister."

"This is crazy." Amanda felt as if she'd fallen asleep and woken up in someone else's life. "I don't want to be part of a fake betrothal. And I'm darn certain Bradley feels the same." She fell silent. What if it didn't have to be fake? Was it possible Bradley fancied her, envisioned a lifetime with her?

Was such a thing what she wanted?

She thought of her ma, a woman who spent her lifetime pining for a man who had been taken from her. Not much different from pining for a man she couldn't have. She pushed herself up and swung her legs over the side of the bed. "Remember the other day, when you asked me what I would do if I could do anything? Well, earlier today in Yuma, I got this crazy idea."

Quickly she shared her impression of the music hall. How it could be a community magnet for the town. A place for folks to meet and mingle and be entertained. A hall with multiple purposes to meet the townsfolk's needs.

Eventually the two were interrupted by Brody. "It's past

time I take my wife home. Bradley's just outside the room. Is it okay if I send him in? Seems you two have a few things to chat about."

"Give me a minute," Amanda said, well aware she must look a fright, with her hair sticking out all ways to Sunday. She did her best to tidy her hair and pinch her cheeks for color before there was a discreet knock at the door. "Come in," she called.

Bradley entered and set a cup of tea down on the side table, within reach. "I kinda figured you could use this."

"Thank you." She took a sip. Sweet the way she liked it.

Bradley stood awkwardly, a few steps away. "Sorry about everything," he said, which left her wondering just exactly what *everything* referred to.

"You can relax if you think you're being prodded to the altar with a shotgun in your back." Was it her imagination or did he visibly lose some of his tension?

"I told Brody I wasn't a marrying kind of guy."

"So this was his idea, not yours?" Her tone was sharper than she intended. He glanced at her warily, as if sensing a trap.

"He kind of jumped to conclusions over what he saw when we were in the river."

"Jumped to conclusions?" Her voice rose shrilly. "You were naked and kissing me. What other conclusion could a body possibly reach other than my virtue had been compromised?"

His shoulders tightened. His face closed down, lips drawn in a thin line. "Your virtue is intact."

"While my reputation is in shreds," she said. "But then men don't have to worry about things like that. Only women."

He cleared his throat. "I thought we could just ..." He

66

paused. "Until things are a little more sorted around here, maybe we could pretend like we're betrothed. Keep the peace for now. Call things off when the time seems right?"

"Call things off? Do you have any idea what *that* will do to my reputation? Bullet is a small town. No decent man will have me if he believes you tarried with me, then cast me aside. We'll get married all right. In name only. You owe me that much." As her anger grew, her words tumbled over themselves.

"You don't want my name," Bradley said bitterly. "It's not even mine. No one knows what my real name is."

"Bradley Mason works just fine for me. Now if you don't mind, I'd like to get some sleep. It has been a very long day."

Not until Bradley left, closing the door behind him, did Amanda expel the long breath she had been holding. Her heart ached for the small boy inside the man, the boy who had been abandoned and abused, turned into the man who felt undeserving of love.

She believed with every fiber of her being that Bradley was capable of giving and receiving love. He just needed to learn how. Once they were married, they'd have an entire lifetime together to figure it out.

Certainly it would be fun to have Bradley woo her and pursue her, amidst declarations of undying love. But since that wasn't likely to happen anytime soon, she would settle for solving this her own way. Seducing Bradley to the point of madness.

Amanda and Laura were already in the carriage, set for a trip into town, when Brody appeared. "Where are you off to?"

"Into town," Laura said. "I need a few things from the store and I thought I'd pick up the mail at the same time."

Brody pursed his lips. "I don't like you setting off alone."

"I'm not alone. I have Amanda for company. Don't go getting all over protective on me all of a sudden. We talked about this before we got married."

"It's a husband's job to protect his wife."

"Protect. Not smother," Laura said smoothly as she picked up the reins.

She sighed. "Brody, you know I am more than capable of a little trip into town without you or one of the boys tagging along."

"I also know what Hawkes is capable of."

Amanda knew they were remembering the butchered cat Hawkes had delivered at their wedding celebration. "I have my pistol," she said.

Brody snorted and wheeled away. "Lord help us all."

"What did that mean?" Amanda asked, as they started on their way.

"I think it was his polite way of saying he hopes you never need to use it."

Amanda sniffed. "I bet no one talks to Henrietta that way."

"Having met Henrietta, I am willing to bet she is an excellent shot. Among other things."

"In any event," Amanda said, "it's nice to get off the ranch. I'm not used to feeling like a prisoner."

"Is that the ranch making you feel trapped? Or your unexpected betrothal to Bradley?"

Amanda took her time with her answer. She'd never really had a friend to confide in before. Maybe it was past time she did. "Bradley offered to wait for things to die down, and then release me from our arrangement."

"Is that what you want?"

Amanda shrugged. What did she want? Maybe for Bradley to look at her the way Brody looked at Laura. "When you first met Brody all those years ago, how did you know he was the one?"

Laura's eyes took on a dreamy expression. "I don't know how to explain it. It was sort of what I imagine it feels like to be hit by a bolt of lightning. Just this sure rightness of knowing, this man and I were meant to be together forever. That my life without him would never be complete."

"It's a shame your family interfered. The two of you lost ten years together."

"We're together now and that's all that matters." She cocked her head toward Amanda. "I gather there was no lightning bolt between you and Bradley?"

Amanda let out a pent-up sigh. "Ever since he came here, I watched him from afar. And hoped that one day he'd truly see me."

Laura grunted. "Those Mason men. No slow awakening with them. More like you need to hit them over the head with a shovel."

Amanda giggled. Already she felt better. "I know exactly what you mean."

"I can't wait to see how the work is going at the café," Laura said.

Comprehension dawned. "You don't really need anything from the store, do you?"

"Not really," Laura said. "But I have no idea how Brody would feel if he found out I supplied the funding for the café expansion. I fear he'd want to get involved, and quite frankly he has enough on his plate with everything at the ranch."

As they drew near to Bullet, Amanda saw a colorful traveling caravan set up in a clearing. The sign on the side of the caravan read, *The doctor is in! Potions for whatever ails.*

"Oh, my," Laura said as they drew close.

"What?" Amanda looked to see what was causing her friend consternation.

"Nothing," Laura said. "It's just that's the same kind of snake-oil salesman Brody's mother ran off with when he was a boy. He hates those traveling hawksters who claim they can cure anything from a broken leg to a broken heart."

"Really?" Amanda said, taking a second, closer look as they passed. The back of the caravan opened and out burst a tall, very handsome stranger. His flowing white shirt was unbuttoned, revealing a broad muscular chest. His hair was long and dark, as dark as his eyes when they collided with hers. Amanda quickly looked away.

At the café, things were really taking shape. The outside walls of the expansion were already framed. Georgina had been adamant she couldn't close up for the time it would take to build the addition, so the crew had compromised by building the new part without touching the existing area. Once the new part was complete it would be a simple matter to remove the far wall and blend the new space with the old.

"That new cook you found me is a marvel." Georgina had rushed to their side the second she saw them. "And the new furniture I ordered will really brighten things up." Amanda had never seen the other woman nearly so animated. Abruptly Georgina's face fell.

"What is it?" Laura asked.

Georgina clasped her hands behind her back and stared down at the toe of her boots where they brushed the hem of her gown.

"I saw this new industrial-size stove when I was looking at the furniture."

"So order it," Laura said.

"I'm worried I may never be able to pay you back," Georgina said. "Everything costs so much."

"You let me worry about that," Laura said. "Once the money starts rolling in from the increased sales, you won't worry anymore."

Amanda piped up. "Have you thought about selling ice cream?"

ACROSS THE STREET, Hawkes glared at Sheriff Yates. "How is she managing to suddenly do this big add-on?"

Yates shrugged. "I did what you said. Gave her a list of things to fix. Even tried to pay off the workers so they don't show up, but they weren't having it. Said she pays fair and on time."

"Did you reason with them?"

"If you mean threaten them, the answer is no. I'm the law around here. There's only so much I can do."

"Don't go forgetting who got you elected in the first place."

"I don't, and I'm grateful. But I got other folks to answer to besides you."

Hawkes narrowed his gaze on the construction zone. "Actually, leave things be. Once I own everything in town, I can put the prices up as high as I want. Folks will have no choice but to pay. Bigger café means bigger profits, right?"

"What makes you so sure this place is on the cusp of a big boom? And if that happens and folks can't afford to live here, then what?"

"Do you think I care about what happens to the people around here?"

"You built them a school, didn't you?"

"It's all part of the master plan. And more than that, you don't need to know."

Yates spat on the ground. "Don't like being kept in the dark."

"Trust me. It's for your own good." He glanced across the street and scowled. "What's *she* doing here?"

Yates followed his gaze. "Who? Mason's wife? Appears to have got quite friendly with the owner since she moved here." He looked at Hawkes. "Aren't you the one responsible for her being here?"

"Don't remind me," Hawkes said. "I'm far from done with her yet. Her and all those Mason idiots." He dug his heels into the flanks of his mount and wheeled away.

"Where you going?" Yates called after him.

"Got some business to take care of."

Laura sat before the looking glass, brushing her hair smooth and braiding it loosely in readiness for bed. Brody appeared in the reflection behind her, his hands moving in comforting circles on her shoulders. Her eyes met his through the mirror. "Are you certain you did the right thing, my love? Pushing Bradley at Amanda?"

"When a man's too stubborn to see what's in front of his own face, he needs a little shove."

"You mean like you? All your brothers pretending to woo me in order to make you jealous?"

"I was blind with jealousy," he admitted. "I lost you once. I couldn't bear to lose you a second time."

Laura smiled at her reflection. She had loved Brody since she first laid eyes on him, and even though it had been a roundabout journey, here they were, together at last.

His eyes met hers in the looking glass, heavy with desire. "What were you girls chatting up a storm about in the bedroom when I came in the other day? I swore I saw a twinge of guilt."

"No such thing, my darling. We're just making plans. Girl-type plans that have nothing to do with you."

She turned and stood to run her fingers over his lips. "Something is troubling you, my love. And don't deny it. I know you too well."

Brody hesitated, then nodded. "It's Hawkes. Man has been too quiet lately. I almost wish the cattle poisoning was on his head. It would give me some idea where he plans to hit next."

"You sound very certain there will be a next."

"Sure as the sun rises in the east and sets in the west."

"When are you and the boys going to start building a house for Bradley?"

"Soon as the others get back from moving the next herd."

"You really think moving the cattle by railcar is the right move?"

"It's the way of the future. Our future. And the future of our children."

Laura fell silent. They both knew Hawkes would stop at nothing to ensure there was no future for those who stood between him and the Copper Moon Ranch.

"You're sure you have Amanda's documents some place safe where Hawkes will never get his hands on them?"

"I'm sure. And that, my dear wife, is all you need to know about that."

Laura hid a smile as she nuzzled into his arms. She loved that Brody was so protective toward her, even though she was frustrated by what he saw as "her place".

And while her husband might have his secrets, she had hers as well.

CHAPTER 6

Being betrothed was nothing like Amanda had imagined. Blame it on those fanciful dime novels she read as a teenager, where the couple escapes from under their chaperone's watchful eye and sneaks away to steal a forbidden kiss. A kiss of such passion it leaves the couple fair swooning with desire.

Nothing could be further from reality. Bradley was out of the house long before she opened her eyes in the morning, stayed busy on some distant quarter of the ranch with Brody and the others, only to appear after dark, dead tired. He barely managed to stay awake long enough to eat something and fall into bed.

There was no witty conversation or exchanged glances of shared passion between them. And certainly no opportunity to get Bradley alone and test her seductive powers. Despite her recent trip into town with Laura to check on the café's progress, she was bored. She missed her home. She missed her piano. She even missed her little evening job with the "ladies".

Her life hadn't been fancy, but it had been hers. Her days

to fill as she chose. Four of the Masons had rounded up a herd and headed west, which meant the ranch was about as lively as a tomb.

Laura was napping and no one was around the day she gave into an impulsive idea that had been steadily building. No one questioned her when she saddled a horse and rode toward town.

Perhaps the caravan wouldn't be there. Perhaps the handsome stranger would have packed up his wares and moved on. Her heart sped up as she got closer and spotted the colorful conveyance with its gaudy signage. She slowed down and approached warily. Ashen remnants of a cooking fire sat in the middle of a loose circle of stones.

She reined to a stop, indecision warring within. Perhaps he wasn't here. She could return to the ranch with no one being the wiser. This had been a foolish impulse. Best she leave before—

"I say, there. Good day." The man she had seen on her earlier trip to town appeared from around the corner, casually fastening his trousers. Amanda flushed to the roots of her hair. His shirt was unbuttoned like the other day, muscles rippling with his easy movements as he pushed his long hair back from his face. "Don't be shy. I don't bite." White teeth flashed in his bronzed face as if he'd made a terrific joke.

"I think perhaps I've made a mistake," Amanda stammered, disconcerted when he approached and took hold of the horse's bridle.

"A lot of folks are hesitant when they first come to see me." The man spoke in soothing, hypnotic tones as he stroked the horse's neck. Amanda felt her anxiety recede.

"You passed by the other day," the man continued. "I knew you would be back."

"You couldn't possibly," Amanda said. "Even I didn't know."

"I think you did," he said, gazing up at her. "You're in need of a potion. But not for yourself. For someone else." He continued to observe her in an unsettling way. "Wait here."

He gracefully climbed the ladder-like steps into the back of the caravan, and returned almost immediately. He passed her a small glass vial.

"What's this?" Amanda said, turning it around in her hand.

"My love potion. Slip five drops into his beverage each day. Before you know it, you will be the object of his deepest desire."

"What's in it?" Amanda studied the vial suspiciously.

"That I can not divulge. But I can tell you, it will only work if you believe in the elixir's powers." He released the horse's reins and bowed low from the waist. "I wish you much happiness."

"Wait!" Amanda called after him. "How much do I owe you?"

He flashed her a blindingly-white smile. "Your happiness is payment enough."

HAWKES DISMOUNTED in front of the Cooke house. He hadn't been here since the night he broke in. He'd been disappointed not to find that dumb red head at home. He'd looked forward to roughing her up some. As soon as he got his hands on what he'd come for. He'd had to settle for roughing up the house instead. Not nearly so satisfying.

All these years that dumb bitch of a mother had been lying to him. Her old man's confession wasn't safe in some lawyer's office at all. He should have known she'd keep it close at hand. Of all the rowdies he'd recruited over the years, Cooke had been the most difficult. All his high-falutin' plans for a better life. Choking the breath from the loser had been the most satisfying of the bunch. The one he'd saved for last.

"Mr. Hawkes."

"Sir Percy." Hawkes gritted his teeth and reminded himself to play nice with the British dandy. "Okay if I come in?"

He didn't miss the way the other fellow hesitated.

"My partner and I are in the middle of something."

"Didn't know you had a partner." It was a lie of course. Hawkes prided himself that nothing happened in Bullet without his knowledge. He'd heard all about the Argentinian beauty with her man's wear pants and her haughty attitude. He'd love to take her down a peg or two. But now wasn't the time. He pasted a genial smile on his face as he pushed his way inside. "This won't take long."

"Henrietta Hutton," Percy said. "This is Mr. Hawkes. The man has quite the reputation here in Bullet."

"Make that all of Arizona," Hawkes said. "No point in being modest."

"Apparently not," said the woman as she accepted his hand. Hers was slim and dry to the touch. He took a second to imagine it other places on his person. Whether she liked it or not.

He looked around in interest. A huge unrolled map took up most of the table in the center of the room. It was covered with squiggles he couldn't decipher right way up, never mind upside down. "How's the treasure hunting coming along? I hear you're making some progress."

"We're happy with our findings so far." Percy looked like he'd swallowed something that left a bad taste in his mouth.

"Just wanted to offer up some of my boys. If you need a crew that's good on the end of the shovel."

"It doesn't quite work that way," Percy said. "But thank you for your kind offer."

"If you need some dynamite, I can help you out with that as well," Hawkes said.

"How kind," Henny-Penny said coolly. "We'll be sure and let you know."

"Have a meeting scheduled with some of my investor friends. Hoping you could fix me up with some information about the project. Something I could pass along to them. To help secure their interest, you understand."

He didn't miss the look that passed between the two before Percy spoke up. "We prefer to address potential investors ourselves."

"As I tole you before. That's not the way we get things done here in Bullet. Everything goes through me."

"You've made that most clear."

Hawkes narrowed his gaze, aware the other man was slowly and subtly making his way to the door to show him out. "Don't cotton to folks interfering, if you catch my meaning."

"Abundantly," Percy said, as he grasped the knob and opened the door. "And we do thank you for your interest. Taking the time to stop by and all."

"My pleasure." Hawkes smirked. "My pleasure indeed."

AMANDA HEARD a deep rumble in the distance, almost like thunder. A glance out the kitchen window revealed a cloudless blue sky, so she didn't give it another thought as she returned to the bowl of bread dough she was stirring with a wooden spoon before she turned it onto a floured board.

She punched the ball of dough harder than necessary, then placed the dough into a greased bowl and set it on the back of the stove to rise. She had just started to wash up the dishes when she heard a commotion outside, the gallop of hooves against the hard-packed ground.

She rushed to the front window and pulled the faded curtain aside just in time to see Braydon and Brody lift Bradley down off his horse. Each took an arm and supported Bradley between them.

Amanda flung open the door. Her heart leapt in her throat at the unnatural way Bradley's head flopped limply between them.

"He's conscious, but barely," Brody said before Amanda could open her mouth. They set him down on the settee in the parlor. Brody got a basin of water while Braydon yanked off Bradley's boots.

Amanda gulped as blood seeped from a wound on Bradley's thigh and stained the fabric of his trousers. Braydon pulled out his knife and cut the fabric away to reveal a nasty, gaping gash. Amanda swallowed her nausea and raced for the first-aid kit.

"What happened?" she asked, as she passed Brody the kit. Bradley's eyes were closed, his face ghostly white, as Brody dabbed at the wound to clean it. The basin of water turned red with Bradley's blood and Amanda had to look away.

"Don't rightly know," Brody said. "There was some kind of explosion. Knocked Bradley clean off his horse."

"I know!" Braydon said grimly. "Hawkes has been in the area with dynamite. Must be using tripwire to set off the blasting cap if one of us gets too close."

Brody's mouth thinned with displeasure as he looked up at Braydon. "He's getting bolder."

"Or desperate," Braydon said. "There's something on this ranch he wants to keep us away from. Or keep for himself."

"Pretty extreme way to try and run us off," Brody said. "Dynamite can be dangerous if you don't know what you're doing. Plus, I don't much like the idea of him chasing around here, going wherever he fancies."

Braydon looked grim. "Hawkes doesn't care who he hurts or kills. So long as he gets what he's after. Shame he didn't set his sights on some other ranch."

"He figured the Copper Moon would be easy pickings once my uncle died."

"Should I go fetch the doctor?" Amanda asked. She felt completely helpless as the other two calmly took charge. Brody finished cleaning the injury and doused it with whiskey. Bradley hissed between his teeth as the liquor hit his wound.

"Sorry, brother. This is going to hurt." Braydon threaded an oversize needle with black thread, and soaked both in more whiskey. "Take a breath."

Amanda knotted her hands together at the front of her apron.

"Hold him down," Braydon said to Brody. Mercifully Bradley must have lost consciousness just as the needle probed into the jagged flesh. Still, he thrashed and tried to move under Brody's firm grip as Braydon swiftly and efficiently sewed up the afflicted area.

"Nothing the doc could do that hasn't been done." Brody stood. "What you can do is make sure he keeps still. And doesn't put any weight on that leg." He turned to Amanda.

"You got that fancy schmancy pistol of yours close by, just in case?"

Amanda nodded, wide-eyed. "Where are you going?"

"Back to the explosion site. See what's what." Braydon stood as well. He placed a hand on Amanda's shoulder. "Bradley's tougher than he looks. He'll make out just fine. Rest is the best thing for him right now. Best you can do is keep him still once he wakes."

"What if he hit his head? What if he doesn't wake up?"

"Bradley's got the hardest head of any of us. He'll be okay." As if on cue, Bradley stirred and moaned.

"Give him a little tepid broth when he wakes," Brody said. "It'll give him strength for the healing." Then they were gone.

Amanda had never felt so inadequate. Nothing in her twenty-two years living in Bullet had in any way prepared her to play nursemaid to an injured man. Still, it was a rare treat to study Bradley when he didn't know he was being scrutinized.

His straight dark hair had flopped into his eyes, and she smoothed it back. Did his skin feel unnaturally warm? She pursed her lips as she studied his chiseled features up close. Dark lashes any woman would envy. Sharply-etched cheekbones framed a thin nose and complemented a square jaw pebbled with a day and a half of dark stubble.

He stirred restlessly. His skin *did* look flushed. She fetched a cool, damp cloth and laid it across his forehead. Under her ministrations, his eyes fluttered once then grew still. She thought his breathing deepened.

Amanda kept a silent vigil by his side as the bread rose and eventually made it into the oven. Other than that, she never left him, except to put the pot of broth to warm on the back of the stove, in readiness for when he woke. If he woke. What if he died? She couldn't bear such a thought.

The light outside faded and she lit a lantern for illumination. When she turned back to check her patient, she started. His eyes were open and watching her.

"Goodness," she said, feeling suddenly tongue-tied. "You're awake."

"So it would seem," he drawled.

"How's your head?"

"Hurts like the blazes. What happened?"

"The others said you rode into a trap. Dynamite. Lucky you weren't killed."

"Unlucky for you," he grunted. "You would be rid of an unwanted fiancé."

"Don't talk like that." She perched on the edge of the settee, careful not to jostle his injured leg. "I've been worried sick about you."

"Bread smells good," he said, at last. "What's a fella got to do to beg a warm chunk with butter?"

"Brody said you should have broth to help heal you."

"Brody's not here now, is he?" He took her free hand between both of his, turned it palm up and started to trace random patterns with his fingers. The sensation chased a tingle straight up her arm to lodge someplace near her bosom, which was also growing warm with an unfamiliar tug of feelings. All of her felt suddenly overheated.

"My, but it's warm in here from the oven." She tried to pull her hand free, but instead of releasing her, he reeled her in closer. She placed a hand, flat-palmed, on his chest for balance. Up close, she could see herself reflected in the inky darkness of ebony eyes.

She tried to push away. "Brody says you're to sit still. No moving around and putting weight on that leg."

"I guess then maybe you ought to lie here next to me and make sure I don't move."

She managed to lever herself to her feet. "Let me get you some of that broth."

"Long as you know I'll need you to feed me," he drawled. "Me being an invalid and all."

She caught her breath as she spooned a small amount of broth into a bowl. Bradley was playing with her, jockeying to get the upper hand. Maybe even trying to scare her off. Well, she wasn't about to let that happen. She'd show him how two could play that game.

He'd managed to scooch up to a sitting position, and Amanda took advantage of the move to tuck a pillow behind his back in what she hoped was the way a proper fiancée would take care of her man.

"Aren't you the attentive little thing?" He gave her a lazy smile, as if he knew exactly what she was up to. She bit back a smile. He had no idea just how attentive she could be.

She pulled a small wooden table close and fetched the broth before she seated herself close to him on the settee. First, she tucked a napkin into the front of his shirt, allowing her knuckles to graze the warm, hair-roughened skin of his chest where the top buttons were unfastened.

Next, she raised the spoon to her lips and blew on it, testing it with her own lips before she raised it to his. She felt a stab of excitement knowing his lips rested exactly where hers had been seconds earlier. He slowly sipped the broth, his eyes never leaving hers. The tension in the room mounted as awareness flared between the two of them.

Once the bowl was empty, she blotted his mouth with a second napkin, taking her time as she wiped the rough cloth over his lips, remembering the thrilling feel when his lips claimed hers. She licked her own lips at the memory.

Somehow the napkin slipped away until it was her fingertips outlining the full contours of his lips. Heated blood moved sluggishly through her veins and her breath caught. Her chest rose and fell. Her breasts tingled, swollen and needful beneath her linen blouse.

Eyes never leaving hers, Bradley took the bowl from her hands and set it aside. She squeaked when he picked her up and placed her in his lap, straddling him with one leg on either side of his hips.

"Bradley, your leg. Plus, this isn't seemly."

"Forget seemly." His voice was rough and low. Could that be desire edging his words? "I nearly died."

She sucked in her breath and, her gaze riveted on his, raised her hands to the buttons of her blouse. Despite her show of bravado, her fingers trembled, making unfastening the buttons more of a chore than it ought to be. The only sounds she heard above their breathing was the overloud ticking of the grandfather clock from across the room. Every time the clock ticked, she would remember this moment, Bradley's eyes glowing with desire, following her every move.

CHAPTER 7

Bradley lay on the settee feeling sick in more ways than one. He couldn't open his eyes, couldn't look at Amanda. He was too disgusted with himself. He was aware of her moving around. After what felt like forever, he heard her soft footfalls on the steps as she went upstairs.

When he was certain she was gone he opened his eyes, awash in total shame. All his life he'd made a point of staying away from virgins.

Until this time.

He'd known she'd be a virgin. Knew it was wrong. Knew she was seeking something he didn't have it in him to give.

Braydon came in a few moments later. He looked around. "Where's Amanda?"

"Went upstairs."

"Hmmph," was all Braydon said before he started banging around in the kitchen. "Did you eat yet?"

"Amanda fed me some broth earlier."

Braydon glanced over at him. "Holy, man! What have you been doing?"

"Nothing. Lying here like an invalid."

"You're bleeding again."

Bradley glanced to the few tell-tale red spots on his otherwise pristine white bandage. "Had to go take a leak," he said, not meeting Braydon's eyes. "What did you find out about the dynamite?"

"Whoever set that charge knew what they were doing."

"Any chance it could have been Percy? Trying to blow something up in hopes of finding his precious lost treasure?"

"I admit I don't trust that guy." Braydon sat down at the table and started shoveling in forkfuls of stew. "Or his mouthy little assistant. Might go have a chat with the two of them."

Bradley propped himself up and swung his legs over the side of the settee. "I'll come with you."

"Forget it. You won't be getting on a horse for a while."

"Bollocks," Bradley said. "If we were in the middle of nowhere and I had to travel, I'd be on a horse."

Braydon looked over his head toward the stairs. Without following his gaze, Bradley knew Amanda had come back down.

"You're fired," Braydon said teasingly as Amanda joined them.

She appeared a lot more composed than he felt until a faint flush stained her cheeks. "Is the bread that bad?"

"It's delicious." Braydon was using his last slice to mop his stew plate. "I mean as a nurse. This guy is bleeding again." Amanda flushed an even deeper red.

"You know him. Impossible to get him to sit still." Her hands shook slightly as she reached into a drawer.

"Where you taking that?" Bradley watched as she wrapped a loaf of bread in a clean tea towel.

"Over to Brody and Laura."

Bradley grunted. Was she racing over to confide in her friend? Surely, she wouldn't tell Laura what had happened between them.

The second the door closed behind her, Braydon turned on him. "Now what have you gone and done?"

Bradley's jaw clenched. "Don't know what you're on about. Think I could have a bowl of stew and a chunk of bread?"

"Get it yourself." Braydon stomped out and took a seat on the porch.

Bradley did just that and hobbled onto the porch with his meal. He seated himself as far from Braydon as possible and propped his injured leg on the railing.

"I mean it, Bray. I'm going with you when you talk to Percy. I want to find out if he's the one responsible." He indicated his leg.

Braydon pushed himself to his feet. "Suit yourself. You always do."

Bradley sat there alone staring off into the dusk. Yup, he was a shit. Not nearly good enough for Amanda. Not nearly good enough to be part of this family.

"COME IN." Laura opened the door, clearly happy to see her.

"I hope it's not too late. I made some bread and thought you might like a loaf."

"You're a darling. It sure is nice to have another woman around. I can't wait till you and Bradley live next door. Brody says they'll start building when the others get back."

It had been less than three months since the wedding. Amanda looked around, admiring the way Laura had turned a stark new cabin into a homey place that looked like it had been occupied forever. Crisp curtains framed the windows. Plump cushions dressed up the settee and easy chair. Two framed samplers added a splash of color to the wall behind them. "Where is he? Brody, I mean."

"He's down at the river getting cleaned up." Laura wrinkled her nose. "He knows he has a much better success rate if he doesn't smell like horses and cattle."

Amanda flushed and looked away.

"What's wrong?" Laura caught Amanda's chin in her hands and angled her face toward her.

Amanda nearly choked on the lump of emotion in her throat. Clearly, she wasn't cut out to be the wife and homemaker that Laura was. "I just don't know that Bradley and I are meant to be together. Especially how it got forced on us. Him, really." She straightened. "Besides. I can't stop thinking about what we were talking about the other night. The music/dance hall idea."

Laura clapped her hands together in delight. "I hoped you still felt that way. I truly think it's brilliant."

Amanda wished she had some of Laura's confidence. "You really believe something like that could work? I keep coming up with ideas for new things that could be hosted there to benefit the entire town. Whether it's performances or community dances, or places for youngsters to explore their talents. Is it all just a pipedream?" She finished in a rush.

"I think it is just what Bullet needs. A place so folks wouldn't need to go to Yuma for entertainment."

"I can't do it by myself," Amanda said flatly. "I'll need a partner."

"I am quite certain that can be arranged."

"Truly?" Amanda could barely believe her good luck. The opportunity to be fully independent, to be making a difference in her town. Who needed to get married? Especially to a man who would rather stay a bachelor.

"Really. Can I share a secret? Promise it stays in this room."

"I promise," Amanda said.

"It's early days, but Brody and I are expecting a baby," Laura said.

Amanda smiled widely. "I should have guessed. You have that glow about you."

Laura placed a finger to her lips. "I haven't told Brody yet. He has a lot on his mind right now, and I know he would just worry extra if he knew."

"You can count on me."

"And you can count on me. I love your dance hall idea. It's high time women started having a positive influence in this town."

RANDALL WAS DOWN at the docks with his foreman, checking off the manifest of the newly arrived steamboat, when Don Lucas came riding up at a clip and reined to a stop, inches away. "Can I help you?" Randall asked mildly as the Mexican dismounted.

"We need to speak. Somewhere in private."

Randall passed the clipboard to his foreman. "Can you finish this?"

"Yes, boss."

"In here." Randall ushered Don Lucas into the messy cubbyhole that contained a paper-strewn desk and one sad chair. He turned and faced the other man, masking his displeasure with a mild tone. "You know I prefer doing business at my club."

"It's in both our best interests that no one knows about this meeting." Don Lucas inclined his head. "Is your man trustworthy?"

Randall shrugged. "As much as anyone. I pay him well to keep his mouth shut."

"I suspect we have a problem with Hawkes," Don Lucas said.

Randall pursed his lips. Personally, he didn't care for most of the unsavory characters he was forced to do business with. Such was the lot of any self-made business man who cut a few corners from time to time. He didn't trust Hawkes either, but at this point, he needed him. "In what way?"

"He claims everything is purely business. But when it comes to the Masons, I believe his feelings are far too personal. And are clouding his judgment."

Randall crossed his arms over his chest. "I assume you're not just talking for the sake of it."

"You sold him dynamite, correct? Ostensibly for use in our mining operations."

"And if I did?"

"Allow me to tell you he is using it for his own purposes. In ways designed to raise a red flag with the locals."

"Go on."

"He assures us the deed to the ranch is as good as in his pocket, yet it appears to me no different from one year to the next. Always a delay. Always an excuse."

Randall took his time before he answered. "I know you and I both have a vested interest in the copper, Don Lucas. But truth is, we tend to do things different around here than the way you might conduct business in Mexico."

"I understand far more of the 'American way of business' than either you or Hawkes give me credit for, my friend. Believe me when I tell you I won't be played for a patsy."

Randall shrugged. "There's still time for Hawkes to deliver. Let's give him the benefit of the doubt." He could tell from the other man's expression that Don Lucas wasn't pleased with his answer. Randall didn't care. Wasn't his job to appease the Mexican. If he didn't trust Hawkes, he trusted this greaser with his put-on airs even less.

ALTHOUGH IT HAD to be painful for Bradley to hobble around, it was plain as the nose on Amanda's face that he was avoiding her like the plague. He wasn't able to be out helping the others on the ranch, which didn't stop him from making himself scarce every day after breakfast. As she collected the eggs, Amanda reached into her apron pocket and touched the cool glass vial of the elixir.

Maybe using it would be a mistake. Clearly Bradley had no desire to spend time with her. What if the elixir worked its magic, only to have the spell wear off over time? Leaving her more miserable than ever, having known, briefly, how it felt to have Bradley love her. Was it better to be loved for a short time and lose that love, or never be loved at all? Her father loving her mother had only left poor Ma miserable without him.

She made her way across the yard to the ranch house. She really ought to go home. She couldn't stay on the ranch forever, looking for ways to keep busy. With Henrietta and Percy happily ensconced in her own home, perhaps she should take advantage of that fact and go on a trip. Now that the rail line was operating, overland travel was much easier than it used to be. She'd never seen the ocean. Laura had told her tales of the mighty Pacific, although the west coast sounded rather primitive. Maybe she ought to head east instead.

"I might go on a trip," she told Laura over one of their innumerable afternoon pots of tea.

"But what about Bradley?"

Amanda shrugged. "Have you seen the way he avoids me?"

Laura didn't deny her words, just blew on her tea to cool it. "What about the music hall?"

"I'm not giving up on the idea," she said. "Just thinking I need a little break from Bullet and everything that goes on here. With Ma gone there's really nothing holding me here."

"Not even your friends?" Laura asked softly.

"You and I will always be friends. It's not like I'll stay away forever." She gave Laura's stomach a gentle pat. "I fully intend to be around to see what sort of a holy terror the next generation of Masons turns out to be."

"Who's a holy terror?" Brody came in on the end of the conversation. Amanda's startled gaze flew to Laura, who chimed in quickly.

"Seems Bradley is being a tad beastly toward Amanda. She's talking about taking a trip."

"Yes." Amanda stumbled to her feet. "I'm starting to feel I've outstayed my welcome here." Her apron caught on the edge of the table, and she gave it a tug. To her horror, the vial of elixir popped from her apron pocket and rolled across the floor to land at Brody's feet.

He bent down to pick it up. "What's this?"

"No... nothing," she stammered.

Brody's eyes narrowed. "Looks like some hocus-pocus potion from that traveling quack who stopped outside Bullet."

Amanda swallowed heavily and stared down at her feet, wishing the floor would open up and swallow her.

He glanced over at Laura. "Do you know anything about this?"

Amanda grabbed his arm. "She doesn't. I went alone. It was silly, and I regretted it immediately."

Brody held the vial up to the light. "What's this miracle cure supposed to accomplish?"

"Make ... make Bradley fall in love with me," Amanda said, low-voiced, realizing how ridiculous the notion sounded. As if some elixir had such power.

"It's still full," Brody said.

Amanda nodded. "It was foolish. Wishful thinking. Nothing can force another person to love you, and I know that."

"So you're done with this then?" Brody walked to the sink and uncapped the vial.

Amanda nodded.

Brody tipped the contents into the sink. There was a hiss of steam as the elixir hit the smooth enamel finish.

"What the—?" Brody's eyes widened in disbelief. Amanda rushed to his side and peered into the sink. A patch the size of a silver dollar had discolored the enamel.

Amanda clapped her hands to her mouth in horror. The sink had been Laura's pride and joy. It was the latest built-in model, forged from steel with a skim of enamel that made it easy to wipe clean. "I'll buy you a new sink," she said.

"Hang the sink!" Brody strode across the room and reached for his gun and holster.

"Where are you going?" Laura said.

"Off to talk to a man about a potion."

"Brody, please don't go." Laura caught his arm beseechingly, but he shook it off.

Amanda's legs felt like jelly. Shakily, she lowered herself into the chair.

Now she'd caused trouble between her best friend and her husband. All because of one stupid, impulsive act.

"I'm sorry," she whispered as the door slammed behind Brody.

"I just hope he takes one of the others and doesn't go hightailing off there alone."

"Did his mother really run off with someone in a caravan much like the one we saw?"

"So goes the story."

"Bradley's mother left her newborn on the steps of a church," Amanda said. "Small wonder he thinks poorly of women."

Laura reached across the table and squeezed her hand. "We'll just have to make sure we raise the next generation of Mason men in a secure and loving fashion."

Amanda took a breath. No point telling Laura there would be no "we". Not one that encompassed her and the Masons.

Brody arrived back a short time later. He strode to Laura's side and swept her into his arms. "I'm sorry, love. That was a stupid thing to do. My emotions got the best of me. I promise it won't happen again."

"I should be going." Amanda stumbled to her feet.

"What happened?" Laura asked Brody.

"The tinker was long gone. His kind never stick around for long in one place." Brody turned to Amanda. "Consider yourself lucky you didn't make Bradley ill, or worse yet, kill him with that concoction."

Amanda lowered her head and nodded. "I know."

"Give him time," Brody said, his voice softer now. "He'll come around eventually."

"You mean like you did?" Laura said teasingly.

Brody made an unintelligible sound.

"The church social is coming up," Laura said to Amanda. "Please stay until after that. We're all planning on going."

"I don't think Bradley will want me there," Amanda said.

Brody and Laura both spoke at the same time. "Too bad. We want you there."

In the end, Amanda couldn't beg off the church social if she wanted to. These were her people. The choir. The congregation. The Reverend Black. They'd expect to see her there. And by now, everyone would have heard of her betrothal to Bradley.

She and Laura spent days preparing picnic food to take, including baking cakes for the cakewalk. At one point Brody popped in and stuck his finger in the bowl of icing, to be unceremoniously shooed back out with Laura brandishing a wooden spoon.

Laura stood back admiringly. "Our cakes will be the most beautiful ones there. And the first ones chosen."

"I hope so," Amanda said. On their last trip to town, she and Laura had stopped at the General Store and purchased a bag of gumdrops. Laura had made a colorful base around her cake, while Amanda had picked out all the red ones and fashioned a heart-shape on the top of hers, secretly hoping Bradley would not only win her cake, but realize he had her heart as well.

"Ma and I used to make a cake every year to donate, praying it wouldn't be the last one picked." She sighed at the memory of the good-natured competition among the other ladies in town. With Ma gone, it was fun to be doing this with a friend her own age.

At last the big day arrived. The buckboard was loaded.

Brody sat up front with Laura next to him. Amanda was behind them on the second seat. Braydon, on horseback waited alongside them.

"What's the hold-up?" Braydon said, pacing next to the fully loaded buckboard where Brody was holding the reins.

"Waiting on Bradley," Brody said.

Amanda looked down and pleated her skirt between her unsteady fingers. Why did she feel it was her fault Bradley wasn't here yet?

Just then Bradley limped over from the direction of the barn. "Hurry up, man," Braydon said impatiently. "We're going to be late."

"I figured someone ought to stay behind," Bradley said. "Keep an eye on things here."

Amanda saw Brody's hands tighten on the reins. "We're a family. We show a united front. Now climb in."

Amanda could tell from the way a muscle jumped in his jaw that Bradley wanted to argue but apparently thought better of it. Favoring his sore leg, he hauled himself into the wagon just as Brody pulled on the reins and the wagon lurched forward. Bradley all but fell into Amanda's lap.

"Sorry," he mumbled as he settled himself in the spot next to her.

She gave him her primmest look. "I hope this won't be too much of a chore for you today. Pretending to be happy you and I are betrothed."

His chest rose and fell in a weighty sigh. "I'll do my best not to embarrass you."

She swept her skirt to one side. "I'd appreciate that."

~

As THEY TRAVELED, the uneven road kept throwing them against each other and Bradley hoped Amanda didn't think he was doing it on purpose. He snuck a sideways look at her prim profile, wondering just how he got himself into these predicaments. Painful as it might be, he owed it to Amanda to put on a good show. By the time they reached town, he had himself well in hand. Today was for Amanda.

They arrived at the park, where it seemed the entire town was in attendance. Blankets were spread around the park's perimeter in a colorful rainbow. Infants slumbered in the shade of the many umbrellas that dotted the landscape.

While the boys unloaded the wagon, Amanda and Laura took their cakes over to the cakewalk area, where numbered squares were laid out in a circle around a big table of cakes. Later today, folks would purchase tickets to walk around the circle. When the music stopped, a number would be drawn and whoever was standing on that square had their pick from the cakes. None of the women wanted theirs to be the last cake chosen.

"Nice of you to join us."

Amanda sighed as she was accosted by one of her least favorite people from the choir. Sissy had a prissy, tight mouth and an accusing gaze, which at this moment was raking across Amanda's cake as if she'd like to push her fist in the middle of it. "I suppose you've been busy out at the ranch with your intended." She skewered Amanda with a mean look. "When are the banns being read?"

To her surprise, Bradley came to her rescue, looping his arm across her shoulders in an affectionate gesture. "Had an accident recently," he told Sissy. "Amanda and I are holding off on making plans until I'm fully healed. Isn't that right, sweetheart?"

Amanda was so shocked she couldn't do anything other than nod.

With a sniff and a twitch of her skirts, Sissy took herself off to find someone else to torment.

"Are your friends all like her?" Bradley asked.

"No friend of mine," Amanda said. "I try to stay out of her way."

"We're set up over here." Bradley took her hand and led her to join the rest of the family. His grip felt big and warm and comforting.

"I need to take my cake over there first."

"I'll come with you."

Amanda was well aware of the looks they received as they crossed the park, Bradley by her side, his usually hurried gait slowed down by his limp, which suddenly seemed more pronounced.

"Angling for viewer sympathy?" she asked dryly, as she set her cake down next to the others on the table."

"If I have to be here, I figure might as well give folks something to talk about."

"Other than us, you mean?"

"The way I see it, they're going to talk anyway." He pulled her close and tipped her chin up so he could gaze into her eyes. Amanda's breath caught, but before anything further happened, they were interrupted by Reverend Black from the church.

"Amanda. Will you be able to help us out later?"

"What do you need?" She turned toward him, trying not to feel deflated that the moment with Bradley gazing down at her as if he cared about her was gone.

"The cake walk is our big fund-raiser. Do you mind playing the piano for it?" He waved a hand toward the gazebo where a small upright piano held place of prominence.

"Who moved it?" she asked, worried it might sound awful and affect her playing.

"Teddy and his sons. Don't worry. We've had it tuned, as well, after the move. The tone is perfect."

"Of course," Amanda said. "It would be an honor."

"I thought we'd start things off today with a couple of hymns."

Amanda gave Bradley a regretful look. "I'll see you over there afterward. Save me some potato salad." He gave her a rakish salute and made his way to where the others were gathered. Amanda watched him join the Masons and wondered if she would ever fit in with them or anyone else.

Dutifully she followed the reverend up the gazebo steps to where the piano waited. He passed her a hymnal open to the songs he had chosen. The choir was assembled next to the gazebo. Sissy stood front and center, and gave Amanda a gloating, self-satisfied look that Amanda chose to ignore. She situated the piano bench to her liking and, at a signal from the reverend, began to play.

The reverend frowned as the social-goers in the park continued to chatter among themselves. He broke things off after two hymns.

"Thank you, Amanda. Go and enjoy your picnic."

As usual, she made her way alone through the crowd. Then Bradley rose and limped over to meet her and she no longer felt alone. Could this possibly work? Could she become Mrs. Bradley Mason? Be part of this loud, boisterous family?

Her thoughts were interrupted by the reverend's voice amplified by a megaphone. She dutifully bowed her head as the reverend recited the mealtime blessing, happy to see that Bradley followed suit. A low murmur of "amens" rippled through the park when the blessing was finished, followed by the delighted sounds of hungry people filling their plates.

From a distance, out of sight, Hawkes watched the proceedings through a spyglass, a scowl on his face. "There will be none of this nonsense once I own this town and everyone in it."

CHAPTER 8

After everyone finished eating, Amanda joined Laura on the blanket. Close by, youngsters raced about, dodging between the blankets, as neighbors mingled, chatting in small groups. "I'm really glad you came," Laura said.

"Me too," Amanda said. "It's nice to feel part of things." On the far side of the park someone had set up games of ring toss for the children and horseshoes for the menfolk. Excited children of all ages were lined up at a booth selling balloons.

"Do you ever wonder why the men always break off and have their own conversations apart from the women?" Amanda asked.

Laura laughed. "Because what they do is so much more important than women's work?"

"So they think," Amanda said, wondering what kind of response she might get from the locals if plans for the music hall ever got off the ground.

"There's Georgina." Laura waved. The café owner waved back and veered in their direction.

As Georgina drew close, Amanda tried not to stare. For

as long as she could remember, the other woman appeared far older than her years due to exhaustion and overwork. Today she looked positively youthful, sporting a new, far more flattering hairdo than her usual tight bun.

Laura moved over and patted the blanket next to her, inviting Georgina to join them.

"Thanks," Georgina said. "I was selling tickets for the cake walk and I'm happy to report they are all sold out." She looked at Amanda. "I think the reverend is anxious to get started before the natives grow restless."

Amanda rose. "I guess that's my cue."

She stepped carefully between blankets, dodged distracted youngsters, and finally reached the gazebo, where the reverend was pacing and wringing his hands.

"There you are, Amanda. I couldn't see you in the crowd." He signaled to a man standing at the cake table, who picked up the megaphone.

"Gather round, folks. The cake walk is about to start."

As Amanda settled at the piano, dozens of hopefuls raced up and situated themselves on the colored squares around the cake table. Cued by the reverend, she began to play the simple tune "Pop Goes the Weasel", which was easy to stop and start and familiar enough for the children to sing along.

Good-natured boos and cheers rang out as, each time the music stopped a winning number was announced, the cake display was studied and choices were made. When the final number was called, a gale of laughter broke out among the nearby observers. Amanda looked over to see what was so funny. There in the middle of the table stood her cake, smashed into pieces.

The final winner dramatically threw his hands in the air and skipped away empty-handed. Stunned and hurt,

Amanda bit down hard on her lower lip as Sissy delivered a self-satisfied smirk from the other side of the table.

Suddenly, Bradley was by her side.

"Where did you come from?"

"Don't pay any mind," he said, low-voiced. His fingers traced a soothing circle against her shoulders. "Play something lively and fun to distract everyone."

Amanda blinked, swallowed and nodded before she swung into a lively rendition of "Oh, Dem Golden Slippers". Bradley started clapping his hands in time to the music. One by one, the Mason clan joined in. Soon the entire park was clapping and singing the lyrics.

The impromptu concert didn't end there. Cheers and whistles from the onlookers encouraged Amanda to play tune after tune. Folks took to their feet. Husbands swung wives around, while toddlers took part standing on their fathers' feet and being shuffled around in time to the music.

When she finally stopped playing and looked over at the cake table, nothing remained of her ruined cake. Not even the crumbs.

Amanda stood and took a bow amid cheers and accolades. She and Bradley descended the gazebo steps, which seemed to be the cue for folks to begin packing up their picnic remains, along with their families.

She turned to Bradley and caught his hand in hers. "Thank you," she said gratefully.

"Sticking up for each other is what we Masons do."

Partway back to where the rest of the family was starting to pack away their picnic, Bradley and Amanda had their way blocked by a trio of men who had clearly been imbibing a little too freely this afternoon. Amanda didn't recognize any of them as local.

"Hey girlie, nice music," one of them said, weaving slightly.

"Play almost as purty as that little gal at Zara's," slurred a second.

Amanda felt Bradley tense. He rested a possessive arm across her shoulders.

"Glad you enjoyed the show, fellows. Now if you don't mind, you're blocking our path."

The man closest squinted up at Bradley as if he was having trouble focusing. "I know you."

"Me too," said the first man. "He's that guy gots no name and no birthday. The boy nobody wanted."

"Everybody gots a birthday. Otherwise you never got birthed."

"Maybe that's his problem. He was hatched." The three of them laughed uproariously as they turned and stumbled away.

"Don't listen to drunks," Amanda said. "They don't know what they're saying."

"Except when it's true," Bradley said darkly.

As if he sensed trouble, Braydon headed toward them. "Everything okay?" he said as he reached their side.

"Why wouldn't it be?" Bradley said shortly.

"Cause those guys usually mean trouble."

Amanda sensed the tension between the two men. "I'll go help pack up." When she glanced over her shoulder, she saw Bradley in a heated discussion with Braydon.

Brody saw it too. He started toward them until Laura's hand on his arm stopped him. The concern on Brody's face was echoed on Laura's.

"Is everything all right?" Laura asked.

"Far as I know," Amanda said, suddenly overcome with

the need to be alone. "You all go along without me. I'm going to stay at my own house tonight."

"Are you sure?" Laura asked.

Amanda nodded.

"Enjoyed the music," Brody said, attempting to break the strained silence that settled between them.

"I'm glad you liked it." Amanda turned and walked away, resisting the urge to break into a run. Her home wasn't far, and suddenly it felt like the most welcome refuge in town.

Henrietta and Percy looked askance at her when she let herself in.

"I say," Percy said. "Everything all right?"

Amanda resisted the urge to yell "no" and stamp her foot. She was sick of people asking that. Things had not been all right for some time now. "Of course," she said, smoothly. "I just ... I just came to get a few things."

Clearly, Henrietta wasn't buying it. She rose and took Amanda's hand. "We're really good listeners. Why don't you tell us what's wrong?"

Confiding in others didn't come easy, but for once it felt good to unburden herself. "I feel like I've made a terrible mish-mash of things," she said. "And poor Bradley is taking the brunt of it, all because of me."

BRADLEY'S LEG was still stiff as he mounted up and followed Braydon into town. Amanda had arrived earlier this morning and whisked Laura into town on some mysterious "ladies' errand". Brody had shaken his head as he related this fact, as if puzzled how their happy bachelor-ranch existence was slowly being eroded by the fairer sex.

"I'd like to get this vendetta with Hawkes settled once

and for all," Bradley told Braydon. "See Amanda safely back in her own home, and—"

"And what?" Braydon gave him a look that clearly saw too much. "Get her to let you off the hook?"

"More like encourage her to find some guy who deserves her. Someone she can count on."

"So be that man," Braydon said.

Bradley fell silent. Easy for Braydon to talk.

"You're not the only one who doesn't know who gave birth to you, you know."

Bradley tensed. Braydon's words closely echoed his own dark thoughts. "At least you grew up in a real home. Surrounded by people who cared." He knew he sounded defensive. Lots of days the bitterness won.

"Surrounded by whores and drunks is more like it," Braydon said darkly. He slanted Bradley a look. "One of those women who 'cared about me' took me into her bed when I was twelve. Made me keep it a secret. Made me feel like what happens between two people is dirty and shameful. The others threw her out when they found out about it. But by then the damage had been done. I used and hurt every woman I was with from that time on. I knew it wasn't right, but I couldn't seem to stop. Conditioned, I guess." He let out a breath, stared off into the distance. "Worst of all, they let me. That's why I get so mad when I see the way you treat Amanda. Sweet, innocent thing has always had eyes for you. Shouldn't be asking a lot for you to love her back rather than take advantage of those feelings."

"You're right. I'm a cad." Bradley kicked his horse into a gallop and paid for it with a stabbing pain slicing through his sore leg. A pain he welcomed. A pain he deserved.

He pulled up outside of Amanda's family home with Braydon close behind. They had barely dismounted when the door opened and out came Percy's cohort, name of Henrietta or something like that. She was nothing like any woman Bradley had seen before, and from the look on Braydon's face, he felt exactly the same.

Beneath her foreign-looking black hat, her hair flowed freely down her back, raven's-wing dark against the crisp white of her man-style shirt. The masculine look didn't end with her shirt either, for she was wearing what looked like a pair of men's breeches, hugging her hips in a way that was almost indecent, tucked into high, shiny brown boots.

Braydon sounded as if something was caught in his throat when he spoke. "Looking for Percy," he said gruffly.

"Sir Percy," she said, emphasizing the other man's title, "is out in the field."

"We need to find him. Can you give us some idea where he is?"

She cocked her head and leveled them with a gaze that gave Bradley a chill. As if she saw far more than what was on the surface. "I'll do one better. I'll take you to him. Provided one of you can give me a ride."

"That'd be Braydon," Bradley said, re-mounting with difficulty. "I got me a bum leg."

"What happened?"

"Ran into some dynamite. You or Percy know anything about that?"

She dismissed his words with a shake of her glossy head. "We never use dynamite in our field explorations. Too much chance of inadvertently damaging important historical findings."

"I still want to talk to him," Braydon said. "Hop on." He reached down a hand and hauled Henrietta into the saddle in front of him. Bradley watched her flip her long dark hair back so it brushed Braydon's face. He smiled to himself as

Braydon glowered and clawed it away. Looked like maybe Braydon had finally met his match. No one would get away with treating this lady poorly.

Bradley turned in the opposite direction. "You two go on. I'll meet you at the ranch later."

ALTHOUGH BRODY HAD INITIALLY BALKED at the idea of Laura and Amanda going into town alone, Laura knew how to work her way around him until he thought the entire idea was his. Amanda wondered if she would ever be able to handle Bradley in the same way. Or if she would even get the chance.

"I want to stop by the café and have a word with Georgina," Laura said. "She might know of a suitable building site available in town. Her café is coming along really nicely now that she's expanding and hired extra help."

Amanda's insides warred between excitement and fear. Could she do this? Create a successful music/dance hall in Bullet? What if she failed?

They passed Hawkes's spread without incident. Laura gave the place a passing glance. "Things have been a little too quiet over there, according to Brody. He's wondering about Hawkes's next show of force. Man didn't take kindly to being arrested for his wife's murder."

"Even though the whole town knows he's guilty." If, as Amanda believed, Hawkes had killed her father all those years ago, proving it would be even more difficult. "Bullies are usually cowards," Amanda added.

"Hawkes reminds me of a cornered rattler. Never know where it will strike next. I'll feel better, and so will Brody, once the others are back safe."

They barely found seats inside the café, which was livelier than Amanda recalled seeing in all her years living here. When she had the chance, Georgina joined them. The owner glanced around and gave a satisfied sigh. "Things are ever so much better here now. We've expanded our hours and our menu. Folks really like the new look." She reached across the table and squeezed Laura's hand. "I am ever so grateful to you, Laura."

Laura smiled as she sipped her tea. "It's all good business. Since you know everyone in town, I thought I'd fill you in on what the two of us are thinking on next."

Listening as Georgina and Laura spoke and planned, Amanda felt her excitement grow. Maybe this was possible. Maybe she could be a successful business woman. Maybe she didn't need a husband after all.

BY THE TIME Bradley reached the outskirts of Yuma, his leg was aching something fierce from the jostling gait of his mount. It was more than likely a fool's errand that brought him all this way, but he heard tell the circus was in Yuma, and something made it impossible for him to stay away.

The circus folk had been the closest thing he ever had to a family, and even though it had been years since he left, trading in the nomadic lifestyle for the stability he found at the Copper Moon, he'd never forgotten the refuge the kind circus folks had offered a scared and half-starved runaway.

He saw the big top in the distance. His blood pumped faster and his breathing felt labored as he drew close and dismounted amid the typical organized confusion of the circus being set up. Shouts, cries, and noise from the animals all combined in a familiar jumble that tugged at his memories.

These days the circus moved across the country by train, vastly different from the wagon train days of his past, with many a night spent on the roads between towns, tending the animals.

As he walked toward the lion's cage, he heard the familiar roar of the big cat before he even rounded the corner.

"Hey you! Get away from there. Can't you read the sign? Or are you too stupid to read?"

Some things never changed. Bradley turned to face the ringmaster, sad to see the man was more portly and red of face than years earlier. "Hello, Gus. How you keeping?"

The older man shaded his eyes from the sun and squinted up at Bradley. "Do I know you?"

"You did once."

Gus's wide mouth opened in a huge grin. "Bradley? You used to be so scrawny. What the heck happened?"

"Learned how to cook, I guess."

Gus enveloped him in a huge hug, and the memory of Gus's kindness brought an unwanted moisture to his eyes.

"Aren't you just a sight for these old eyes. You live here in Yuma now?"

"Next town over. Heard you were travelling through and had to pop by for old times' sake."

"Come here. I gotta get out of this heat." Gus led him to some hay bales in the shadow of a wagon. The old man was breathing heavily as he sat down, as if moving was an effort. His face was flushed and dotted with perspiration.

"Jesse give up nagging you about your weight?" Bradley said jovially, to mask his concern.

"Jesse's been gone these past years."

"Gus, I'm sorry. I didn't know."

"Had us a fire. Lost a lot of the old-timers, trying to save the animals and costumes."

Bradley's heart tightened in his chest. Fire had always been one of the circus's worst fears, what with all the flammable materials around. "Tough break."

"It was a big loss." His eyes were suspiciously shiny before he turned back to Bradley. "You look good, boy. It appears settling down agrees with you."

Bradley nodded. "It was time. You'll be glad to know I'm putting all I learned about caring for the animals to good use where I live."

"You always was a smart one. Too smart to make this your whole life."

"Heck, this life here with you saved me." Gus knew more than most people about the abuse Bradley had suffered with his adoptive parents before he ran away.

Gus heaved himself to his feet. "Come on. Let's see who we can find from the old gang. Go show you off."

Together they made the rounds. Some folks Bradley remembered, while others were new to the troupe. What he wasn't expecting was the shocked look on the face of one couple when Gus introduced him to Maria and Eduardo. The husband and wife team went pale, eyes wide with shock. Maria made the sign of the cross, muttering to herself in Spanish.

"Have we met?" Bradley asked.

The woman clutched her husband's arm, then fell to her knees wailing. Gus and Bradley exchange a baffled look. Her husband helped her to her feet, one arm comfortingly around her middle.

Bradley looked over their heads toward Gus, whose

shrug indicated he was as much in the dark as Bradley was. "Where'd they come from?" he mouthed.

Gus stepped toward him and answered, low-voiced. "Understand they've lived all over. They haven't been with us long. Hard workers. Keep to themselves."

Bradley turned away, but the woman caught his arm. He started when she reached up and touched his face, running her fingers over his features as if she was blind. Tears welled up in her eyes. She said something to her husband in Spanish, who grunted, whether in agreement or disagreement, Bradley wasn't sure.

When she spoke, her English was heavily accented. "You are the spitting image of Rosina. Our beautiful daughter. She died the day you were born."

HAWKES HAD BEEN FOLLOWING Percy for some time now. He didn't like the foreigner. Not since Percy had turned on him that day he had Laura Kismet in his sights out on the cliffs. But he believed everyone had their uses. At least for a time.

He had no idea what the treasure hunter fellow was doing out this way, but he'd been up and down off his horse enough times to make Hawkes dizzy. Constantly scribbling something in a leather book he kept in his pocket. They were out near the old salt marshes where there was precious little cover, which forced Hawkes to hang back farther than he liked. He itched to know what, exactly, Percy was up to.

Appeared he wasn't the only one. Suddenly the Brit was joined by a second horse carrying Percy's female sidekick, along with one of the Masons. Hawkes's gaze narrowed. Now, why would those two be wanting to talk to Percy? The gal ought to know exactly what Percy was carrying on about. And Mason shouldn't care.

Hawkes wished he was close enough to hear what was being said, but for now deemed it best he stay out of sight. Mason dismounted and offered the gal a hand down. She ignored him and made her own dismount. Looked to him like the trio was having quite the chin wag. He thought the gal might stay behind with her dandy, but at the last minute, Mason scooped her back up in front of him in the saddle. Finally, the pair left, and Percy was once again on his own.

Hawkes decided there was no time like the present to make a move. Percy didn't even flinch when he showed himself.

"Mr. Hawkes. I confess I wondered how long it might be before you would decide to make your presence known."

Hawkes grunted. The man claimed he could track. Didn't mean he also knew when someone was following him. "What did Mason want?"

"A little matter of some dynamite a couple of them ran into on the ranch. He wanted to know if it was my handiwork."

Hawkes smiled to himself. *Perfect.* A ready-make scapegoat anytime he needed one. Ought to be easy enough to plant some incriminating evidence pointing to the fancy Sir Percival Bloom.

"Now what can I do for you?"

"Showed up to let you know there's no hard feelings. Also, to tell you I have those investors lined up that we talked about."

Percy frowned. "When did we talk about investors? Oh, you mean when I first came to town? Heavens. That ship has long sailed."

Hawkes narrowed his gaze. "You never said nothing

about it being a limited time offer. These things take some time to put together."

"I somehow didn't get the impression you'd be looking to partner with me. Now or in the future."

"You mean because you joined forces with all them others in the witch hunt against me? Me being falsely accused and all."

"I didn't come out for you or against you, Mr. Hawkes. I believe you know that. I'm simply here to find the treasure ship. I want no part of any ongoing feud among the locals."

Hawkes nodded. "If it turns out you need some financial backing down the road, you know who to come to."

He rode away, turning things over in his mind. He needed to find a way to keep an eye on what the foreigner was up to. Make sure he didn't stray anywhere near a certain spot Hawkes liked to keep private.

BLIND FURY PROPELLED Bradley back toward Bullet. He didn't notice the discomfort of his throbbing leg. He didn't feel a thing except the overwhelming need to strike and kill.

When he found the front door to Hawkes's monstrosity of a home locked, he used his good leg to kick in the door. It was heavier than it looked and took several tries, but finally it separated from the wooden frame with a satisfying splinter.

He shouldered his way inside, his bootsteps echoing on the tile floor of an enormous entrance hall that stretched from one end of the house to the other. He turned to his left, pausing to stick his head into every doorway he passed.

Each room he looked in was empty. He reached the end of the hallway, where one last door stood ajar. Bradley tightened his grip on his gun. His pace slowed as he approached what looked like Hawkes's den. His target sat behind his desk with his back to the door. As Bradley entered, Hawkes slowly spun around in his chair to reveal a Winchester resting across his lap. His finger was on the trigger.

"Don't recall inviting any Mason scum to darken my door."

"You raped my mother!"

Hawkes gave a bored yawn. "Which slut was she? Musta bin a greaser, judging from the look of you."

Bradley raised his gun and pointed it at Hawkes's chest. Hawkes rose, seeming unconcerned, and rounded the desk.

"I have to say, you got more balls than that milksop my wife tried to pass off as mine. Maybe you are my seed. Then again, who knows how many gringos your slut mother spread her legs for."

"She was young and innocent. She died because of you."

Hawkes shrugged. "What's a little more spilled Mexican blood? Isn't that right, Denim?'

Bradley felt a blunt blow to the back of his head. The world went black.

CHAPTER 9

After their visit to the cafe, Amanda and Laura stopped at the General Store and picked up some fresh peaches, which Laura confessed she had been craving. When they reached the ranch, they found Braydon and Brody at odds.

"I'm telling you. Bradley should have been back here hours ago."

"Wouldn't be the first time he took off for a spell," Brody said.

"Not without letting us know first." Braydon's mouth was set in a stubborn line.

Brody looked equally stubborn. "What did he say when you left him in town?"

"That he'd see us back here."

Amanda listened to the exchange, a growing dread weighing her down. This was all her fault for throwing herself at him when he was laid up. He'd pretended to be nice to her at the picnic, but truth be told he couldn't bear to be around her.

Soon as he got back, she'd tell Bradley the betrothal was

off. Let him know she had no intention of marrying him or anyone else. And there would be no more talk of building a house on the ranch for them to live in after they were married.

Bradley came to with a start when a dash of cold water hit him full in the face. He sputtered and shook his head to clear his vision. Wherever he was, it was dark, likely someplace underground judging from the dry-dirt, musty smell. He was half-propped against a wall that felt like hard-packed dirt against his back. He tried to move, only to discover his hands were bound behind him and his feet were lashed together at the ankles.

He heard a sound nearby, followed by the flare of light as a lantern was lit. He blinked to try to adjust his sight from pure darkness. The back of his head ached something fierce. He remembered being riled. Riding hard on his way to confront Hawkes.

The veil over his memory lifted. The circus. That old Mexican couple who claimed to be kin. The things they told him about their daughter, and what that bastard had done.

His eyes closed against the memory. His chin hit his chest. Best for everyone if whoever was down here just killed him now and got it over with.

He yelped as the hair on the top of his head was grasped, his gaze forced forward. He faced one of Hawkes's thugs.

"Nice of you to join us, Mr. Mason. I'm afraid I might have hit you harder than I meant to. On account of it's my job to protect the boss. And you pulling a gun on him was not very smart."

It sure as heck wasn't. Even Bradley was willing to admit

that. He hadn't been thinking clear. And likely never would again.

"Mr. Hawkes, naturally, denies your accusations. Claims he has no knowledge of your mother, whoever the unlucky soul might have been."

"Just kill me and get it over with." His mouth was dry. His lips felt swollen.

"Mr. Hawkes anticipated you might not fight, now you know your miserable life is not worth saving. But he has different reasons for deciding to keep you alive. You see, he believes you might be useful. He sent me to ask you a few questions about certain goings on at the ranch."

"Got nothing to say."

From the corner of his eye, he saw the thug begin to remove his thick leather belt. He began to shake. His past roared up, chocking him with painful memories. He squeezed his eyes shut and waited.

"I believe, by the time you and I are finished, you will be begging to spill your guts."

THE NEXT DAY passed with still no sign of Bradley. His absence was made all the more obvious by the return of the others from a successful trip west to deliver the fattened cattle. Their herd had fetched a good price and everyone was in a celebratory mood, dampened only by Bradley's absence.

Amanda witnessed the concern shared by the brothers, overheard the occasional murmured comment from one to the other. They all agreed it wasn't like Bradley to just up and take off without a word. He'd never leave the ranch's livestock without making sure someone else was able to take over.

Brody sought her out later that evening. "Bradley say anything to you, Amanda? Any sort of indication where he might have lit off to?"

She shook her head.

"You two have a fight?"

Amanda swallowed thickly. She wasn't about to confess how she'd thrown herself at him like a shameless hussy and now he couldn't bear to be in her company, even though he'd come to her defense at the church social. "I wouldn't call it a fight."

Brody stuffed his hands in his pockets. "I can't help feeling I might have had something to do with this."

Amanda shook her head. "Don't say that, Brody. Maybe he didn't cotton to being pushed into marriage, but he has a voice. I appreciate you trying to protect me, especially from Hawkes, but I think maybe he felt ganged-up on. Which has to be hard, when you all are the only real family he's known."

Amanda bit off her words. *Family*.

Yesterday at the store she'd noticed a handbill announcing the circus coming to Yuma. Hadn't Bradley said that's where he learned his animal care? Could the circus have been Bradley's family at one point? She opened her mouth to suggest as much, then shut it again. She had no desire to be the object of anyone's ridicule. Or to send the others off on a wild goose chase.

The following morning, she approached Laura and Brody. "Is it okay if I borrow the carriage for a short while today? I need to fetch a few things from the house."

Brody appeared distracted. Clearly Bradley's absence

was having an effect. "Borrow the carriage? Sure. Blake, get the carriage ready. Take Amanda into Bullet."

"That's not necessary," Amanda said. "I'll be— "

Brody cut her off mid-sentence. "No one leaves here on their own. Last thing we need is to be worrying about someone else who didn't return when expected."

And that, Amanda conceded, was that. Brody had final say. She gave Blake a tremulous smile. "Sorry to be a bother."

Since staying on the ranch, she got the impression that Blake was the shy, quiet one of the brothers. She'd heard from Laura that he had learning difficulties, such as not being able to read or write. Not that he was slow. Just different. And smart as a whip with anything mechanical, Laura had said. Brody relied on him a lot around the ranch.

They set off in the carriage, Blake silent at her side. When she asked him about the recent cattle drive to California and how it felt to go by rail, he was polite enough with his one-word answers but not exactly chatty.

When they reached Bullet, he started toward her house. All the boys knew which house was hers because Laura had lived there before she married Brody. She stopped him before they turned down her street.

"Blake, I have a confession to make. I told a small fib. I don't need anything from the house."

He didn't respond, just pulled over to the side of the road and waited patiently for her to elaborate.

"Did you know that Bradley worked with the circus before he met all of you here?"

"Heard tell of that once. Not something he talked about."

"Well the circus arrived in Yuma the other day. It's

possible that's where Bradley was before he disappeared. I think that's where we ought to start looking for him."

Blake gave her a look that surprised her with its depth of acceptance and understanding. "I learned early on to listen to my gut a lot, on account of not being able to read."

Amanda blew out a relieved breath. "You know something, Blake? If I had a brother, I'd want him to be just like you."

He gave her a slow, shy smile, then headed the rig toward Yuma.

～

HAWKES GLARED AT DENIM. "What do you mean he won't talk?"

Denim shrugged. "My guess? Man is no stranger to being beat. He just turns inward. It's like he doesn't even feel it. No reaction at all."

"Hmmm." Hawkes steepled his fingers. "There must be some way he can be useful."

"Want I should kill him?" Denim said.

"Not yet," Hawkes said. "As long as the Mason boys think he's alive, they'll be out beating the bushes looking for him."

"What good does that do us?"

Hawkes grunted at the man's stupidity. Did he have to explain every little thing to the moron? "If they're out looking for him, that means they leave the women folk unprotected."

"Oh," Denim said, as the dim light of understanding went off in his pea-size brain.

"It also means this is the last place they'll look for him," Hawkes said, feeling mighty proud of himself.

"You got a plan, then?"

Hawkes let out a snort. "When don't I have a plan?"

~

THE ATMOSPHERE at the circus seemed like another world: sights and sounds and smells the likes of which Amanda had never been around before. As their carriage approached the site of the big top on the outskirts of town, even Blake looked uncertain as to where to start.

People were dashing about, leading exotic animals from one area to another. Infectious music drifted through the air, over which she heard a roar that sounded as if it came from a very large animal. A group of acrobats were off to one side practicing their routine, cavorting and twisting in what were surely completely unnatural movements.

As the music grew louder, Amanda craned her neck to see it came from a one-man band. She watched in amazed admiration as the musician plied half a dozen instruments strapped to his chest, back and knees. Had this really, at one point, been Bradley's world?

Blake looked as gob-smacked as her. Amanda tugged on his arm and pointed. "What about that man over there? He looks like he might be in charge."

"Or at least knows who is." Blake parked the carriage and helped her down.

"Excuse me," Amanda began. But the man they approached had his back to them and didn't even turn around.

"Tickets go on sale at four. Come back then."

Blake spoke up. "Who's tending the animals? Since Bradley left."

Amanda shot Blake an admiring glance. He certainly knew how to get the right kind of attention. The man stopped what he was doing, turned toward them and cocked his head. "You know Bradley?"

"Good friends," Blake said. "He went missing a few days ago and we're some concerned."

The man blew out a breath and pulled them off to one side, away from the general chaos. "I knew that was bad news; setting out to get worse."

"What news?" Amanda said. "Bradley was here then?"

"Showed up a couple of days ago around noon." His eyes grew misty with emotion. "Always had a soft spot for that boy. He had a real gift with the animals. Never seen anything quite like it. Anyway, the other day Bradley and a few of us old timers were having us a little yarn about the old days. Right before things went a little crazy."

"Crazy how?"

"There's this older Mexican couple that joined up with us a while back. Normally quiet and keep to themselves. Until they caught sight of Bradley. Craziest thing. Next I knew, they were insisting he was their grandson. Don't know what all they said to him, but he lit outta here like the fires of hell was scorching his ass."

"Are we able to speak with this couple?" Amanda asked.

"Sure can. They're over this way." He cleared his throat noisily. "I'm Gus. I'd do just about anything to help that boy. You tell him that when you find him."

If we find him, Amanda thought. But she didn't say the words aloud.

Blake must have been thinking the same thing, judging by the stricken look on his face. "That them over there?" he asked.

"Sure is. Maria and Eduardo."

"Remind you of anyone?" Blake said quietly to Amanda.

She followed his gaze. Swallowed hard. Was it possible

Bradley had learned something about his parentage after all these years?

⁓

"THE COUPLE WORKED for Hawkes back when he was just starting up," Blake reported. From the circus, he and Amanda returned to the ranch immediately and gathered the others together to hear what they learned. "She was the housekeeper, he looked after the grounds, and their daughter was nurse to young Jeffrey."

Amanda was relieved Blake didn't mention the way she had tried to wrench the reins from his hands as they passed Hawkes's ranch, in a desperate move to rescue Bradley. She couldn't stop feeling that this entire situation was her fault. In the end, Blake managed to convince her that rallying the troops made much more sense than going after Hawkes single-handed, which is more than likely what Bradley had done.

"Hawkes was despicable even back then," Amanda said. "It seems the poor girl was afraid to tell her parents when Hawkes forced himself on her. Afraid her pa would kill him and wind up in jail."

Blake picked up the tale. "The family fled one night and tried to hide, but eventually Hawkes found them at a mission where they had taken refuge. The daughter had just given birth to a baby boy and, sadly, didn't survive the birth. The old man and Hawkes had it out. Ended with Hawkes making off with the baby, saying no greasers would be raising a kid with even an ounce of his blood in him." He paused for a breath. "Poor parents were afraid of US law and Hawkes's power, so they buried their daughter and stayed on the move, always looking over their shoulders. When they heard Hawkes was in jail, they thought they finally might be safe."

He looked at Amanda. "Did I miss anything?"

"Just that a few months ago they heard Hawkes was being released and were petrified he might come for them. They didn't want to go back to Mexico, so they hid out with the circus."

"Good detective work," Brody said.

"Thank Amanda," Blake said. "She's the one figured out where Bradley was before he disappeared."

"Now we just need to figure out where Hawkes has him."

If he's still alive.

None of them said it aloud, but it had to be on all their minds.

"I say we just ride over there. Confront him where he lives," one of the twins said.

"Last thing we need is a shoot-out," Brody said. "We need to be smart about this."

Laura spoke up. "There's an underground cellar at the rear of the house. I remember Jeffrey telling me about it the night I first arrived. I thought he was joking when he said Hawkes used to lock him in there as punishment."

"That'll be as good a place as any to start," Brody said. "We'll wait for dark, then head over there. Blake and Braydon, you two will ride with me. Benjamin and Barron, I want you both to hang back near the road and keep watch. Bishop, you stay here with the ladies."

Bishop opened his mouth as if in protest but, at a look from Brody, seemed to think better. "Sure, Brody."

The men scattered. Laura gave Amanda a sympathetic look. "Don't worry. They'll find him. They'll get him back."

~

BRADLEY CAME to in the pitch black, a dull ache in his skull, lying on what felt like cold earth. Underground. Was he in a grave? He might as well be. He might as well be dead as be the spawn of that devil seed. He wished he was dead.

He had no feeling in his hands or his feet. His leg ached as bad as his head. He had no idea how long he'd been here or if Hawkes had left him for dead. It didn't matter that no one knew where he was. He couldn't look any of them in the face ever again.

With him out of the way, sweet Amanda would meet someone else. Someone who deserved her. Someone who would treat her the way she deserved to be treated. He was no better than the wild animals in his care with the circus.

Memory of the way he had despoiled Amanda made him wretch in disgust, but nothing came up save the dry heaves. He closed his eyes and wished for glorious oblivion to take him.

Of course, no such thing happened. Instead, an overhead hatch creaked open, letting in a sliver of silver light. The moon? He let out a resigned sigh. Maybe this time his tormentor would finish what he started. Put him out of his misery once and for all.

He blinked as his eyes slowly adjusted from the darkness to the faint illumination thrown by that chink of light. He could make out the shadowy rungs of a ladder against the far wall. See the dark bulk of someone starting to descend.

"Bradley, you down here?"

Damn. It was Brody!

He debated staying silent. Maybe Brody would leave. Then sanity prevailed. Brody and the others were putting themselves in danger for him.

"Over here," he said in a rusty voice even he didn't recognize.

His memory stirred. Captured something he'd over-heard during one of Hawkes's thugs' interrogation visits.

"Leave me!" he said. "Get back to the ranch. That's where Hawkes is headed."

"Hang tight." He heard a low murmur from above, then a faint flurry of activity followed by silence. For once, maybe someone had listened to him.

Moments later, the chink of light widened enough that he recognized one of the twins shinnying down the ladder.

He tried rolling to a sitting position but his limbs refused to cooperate. "Where are the others?"

"Headed back. Can you stand?"

"Untie me, and I'll let you know."

AMANDA SIGHED and set her book aside. She must have read the same paragraph ten times now, and none of the words made any sense. She was starting to hate the grandfather clock and the way it ticked out the minutes in a loudly irri-tating fashion. She vowed never to have such an obnoxious piece of furniture in her home.

In fact, clocks should be banned altogether. How much simpler were the days when people ate when they were hungry, went to bed when it got dark and rose when it got light out? Why this obsessive need to parcel each day into tiny, measurable segments?

Nearby, Laura was knitting what appeared to be a tiny white bootie. Amanda wondered how she could concen-trate. Abruptly Laura pulled out the needles and yanked out the tiny stitches, re-rolling the yarn. Her eyes met Amanda's, and she managed a rueful half smile.

All of a sudden Bishop jumped up and grabbed his rifle. Amanda and Laura both turned to him.

"Heard something outside. Going to check on what it was."

"Are you sure that's wise?" Laura asked.

"Lock the door behind me. I'll be right back."

Amanda picked up her fancy new pistol. The sleek coldness of the handle was a reassuring weight in her hand. Across from her, Laura picked up a second rifle and rose to let Bishop out. The click of the lock sounded ominously loud in the silent room.

Amanda's heart was racing so fast she expected it might burst out of her chest. Realizing she was holding her breath, she forced herself to inhale and exhale in a regular rhythm, aware it did little to slow down the gallop of her heart.

A few minutes later they heard the clump of booted footfalls up the front steps. "Just me."

"Everything all right?" Laura stood, the rifle slack in her hand.

Bishop cleared his throat. "The coast is clear."

Laura tensed, gripping the rifle tight. She whispered to Amanda. "That's code with the boys that something's wrong." No sooner had she spoken than the front door was kicked in, the lock shattered.

Before Amanda had a chance to raise her pistol, Hawkes and half a dozen of his henchmen swarmed into the house, easily disarming the women.

"Well, well. Lookee here."

Amanda would give anything to wipe that smug expression from Hawkes's evil face. "Gotta ask myself what old

Brody Mason might do to get his darling wife back safe and sound in one piece."

He swaggered toward Amanda and pressed the tip of his rifle against her forehead. "And you, Sweet Pea. I think maybe you have something rightfully belongs to me."

CHAPTER 10

Amanda tugged against the tight rope around her wrists, that lashed her to the back of her chair. "I told you before, I don't know where that stupid map is. It was stolen from my house. What have you done to Bishop?"

"Haven't killed him yet. Waiting for Brody and the others so they can watch." He punctuated his words with an evil laugh.

She gnawed her lower lip as Hawkes circled her in a menacing way, as if deciding where to strike. Three of the men had taken Laura to the house where she lived with Brody, leaving Amanda here with Hawkes and the other two. She was worried about her friend. Laura was in a delicate condition. If something happened and she lost the baby, Amanda would never forgive herself.

She never should have befriended Laura, never become involved with the Masons. All would have been fine if she had just minded her own business. She bit her lip so hard she tasted blood, unable to believe how selfish and foolish she had been. Thinking she was so smart, thumbing her nose at Hawkes because of the legacy from her mother.

Her heart rate galloped. Even if she managed to loosen her bonds, she would hardly be able to escape from three armed men.

"What if the others come back?" One of Hawkes's flunkies was starting to sound nervous.

"Shoot 'em on sight. Except Brody. I want him alive. If anyone knows the whereabouts of those documents, it's him. And we have something he cares about deeply." He laughed again, a low, evil sound that chased up and down Amanda's spine and lodged deep in the pit of her stomach.

Without a sound the door flew open, startling them all. In strolled Sir Percy, as if he was out for a walk around the garden.

"I say, Hawkes. Been looking everywhere for you, my good man. Splendid news. We found the ship." He paused, apparently taking in the scene before him for the first time. "Have we come at a bad time?"

Hawkes leveled the barrel of his rifle in the center of Percy's chest. "Get the hell out of here, Bloom!"

Sir Percy made as if to raise his hands in a gesture of surrender. In a motion so fast Amanda blinked and missed it, Percy had twin shooters blasting and Hawkes's two henchmen were prone on the ground, spurting blood. Brody must have come in through the back, for he held a pistol to Hawkes's temple.

"I wouldn't so much as breathe if I was you, Hawkes."

As Brody spoke, Bloom relieved Hawkes of his rifle and collected the weapons that lay scattered across the room

Hawkes turned an unhealthy-looking shade of purple. "I suggest you release me if you ever want to see that pretty wife of yours again."

Brody faced his sworn enemy with smooth confidence. "Oh, Laura is just fine. Seems Percy and his associate saw your men dragging her across the yard and decided to intervene. No shots were fired, but apparently he and Henrietta have both learned some fancy combat moves in their travels."

"This is far from over, Mason."

"And I suggest you think twice before you threaten me and mine."

"You wouldn't shoot me in cold blood in front of witnesses. You'd hang."

Amanda felt the ropes on her wrists being cut and twisted around to see Braydon taking care of her release. "Did you find Bradley?"

"He's okay. Banged up some. Barron is bringing him right along."

After that, Amanda lost track of the comings and goings. The ranch house teemed with activity. Laura showed up and was indeed fine.

Seeing the way she and Henrietta got along, Amanda felt a twinge of jealousy. Why hadn't she been the one to rescue her friend instead of tied up here helplessly, like a heroine in a cheap dime novel? Why couldn't she be dashing and brave and adventuresome like Henrietta?

"You'll have to show me what you did to take that thug down like a bag of dirt," she heard Laura say.

"I'd be happy to," Henrietta said. "I have a few useful tricks up my sleeve."

"A woman never knows when she might find a few tricks helpful," Laura said.

Amanda had never felt like she'd belonged anyplace less than here and now, unable to shake the feeling that she had brought this all on. That her friends had been in danger because of her.

Abruptly the background noise faded away. Amanda

looked up to see Bradley, white and shaken but moving on his own. She tried to catch his gaze across the room, but he wasn't making eye contact with anyone. She hastened to his side, where he still didn't quite meet her gaze but seemed enthralled by something just above her left ear.

"Barron said you were the one who figured out what happened and where I was."

"I'm just so relieved you were rescued. We were worried sick." She bit back the words that were top of mind. How this was all her fault. "What were you thinking, charging in on Hawkes all on your own?"

"Not thinking," Bradley said shortly as he pushed past her and went up the stairs. He moved stiffly, like a man in a great deal of pain, and she hated to think what those monsters had done to him.

It took some time and coordination, but eventually Hawkes and his thugs were tied up and loaded in the buckboard wagon, ready to be transported into town. Amanda milled around nearby as the Masons argued over which of them got the privilege of delivering the lot to the sheriff's office. Laura plucked at her sleeve for her attention.

"I'm worried," her friend said. "Whoever drives off with them won't make it very far."

"What do you mean?"

"I mean they all want Hawkes out of the way once and for all. I overheard several of them discussing all the places the wagon could go off the road accidentally, down a steep ravine, maybe end up in the river."

Amanda glanced around. Were the Masons capable of cold-blooded murder?

"You should let Bradley," she heard Barron say. "You heard that story about Hawkes and the young girl who worked for him. Bradley's mother according to the girl's parents."

"It's all just conjecture," Brody said.

"Sheriff won't do anything. Be just like last time. Hawkes will be free as a bird, soaring in for the kill."

"I thought we agreed," Brody said. "Piece by piece, we destroy the man. A quick, easy death is more than he deserves."

Bradley interrupted. "I'd settle for seeing the job done. However that looks."

"You're not in a frame of mind to decide anything right now." Brody looked tense. Amanda knew he wasn't used to having his authority questioned. Had there ever been a mutiny among the seven of them? They all seemed so close. Had she somehow caused this discord as well?

In the end, the decision was taken out of their hands by the arrival of Sheriff Yates.

"What in tarnation!" the sheriff barked into the confusion. "I hear reports of gunshots coming from this area."

"Self-defense, old man," Percy said. "The ladies were being held against their will."

"I'd get a lawyer if I was you," Hawkes growled from his bound position in the wagon. "It's your word against all of us."

"I am a lawyer. And a bloody good one at that," Percy said, dusting an imaginary spec of lint from his sleeve. "Sheriff, I believe this can all be sorted with relative ease. Away from here, and after tempers have cooled. Luckily, no one was seriously hurt."

The sheriff's gaze darted around the group, as if assessing the general mood. "Don't appreciate a lot of messy paperwork in my county."

"Exactly. You and I are clearly men who think along the same lines."

"How long do you think Hawkes will end up staying in jail this time?" Blake asked Brody as Bloom and the sheriff took charge of the buckboard.

"Same as before. Not long enough."

"I don't want any more of that kind of talk," Laura said. "We've had enough disruptions for one day."

Amanda tried again to catch Bradley's eye, but it was obvious he was avoiding her, limping around on his sore leg like a bear with a sore paw.

"Going to check on the animals," he muttered.

Amanda piped up. "Shouldn't you be resting your leg? How do you expect it to heal?"

"Let him go," Braydon said. "He gets like this sometimes. Fit company for animals only."

"Not even them," Bradley said over his shoulder as the darkness swallowed him.

"I should go home," Amanda said to Laura. "My being here has only made everything worse."

"This is hardly your fault."

Amanda wished she believed that. "It's a bachelor house. Seems I bring the same kind of bad luck as a woman on a ship." She made it sound like a joke, but no one laughed.

Barron spoke up. "You were a big help finding Bradley."

"Glad I could be of assistance."

Laura stood. "Come on, Brody. Let's go home. I have something important to talk to you about."

It didn't take Amanda long to pack up her things. The house was eerily empty when she came back downstairs, except for Blake. He had something metal and greasy taken apart into a million pieces on the table. "Will you take me home in a few minutes?"

Blake didn't look up from the pieces he was squinting at in front of him. "If that's what you want."

"It is." She set her valise down near the front door. She couldn't leave without saying something to Bradley.

She'd done this before, sought out Bradley in the barn, which seemed to be his safe place when the rest of the world got to be too much for him. Her heart felt heavy as she trudged down the straw-strewn corridor until she found him.

"I came to say good-bye."

He straightened to face her. "Don't go on my account. I'll be the one doing the leaving."

"That would be a mistake. This lot is your family. They care about you."

"I don't deserve them." He made a broad gesture with his hand. "I don't deserve any of this. I'm sorry that I sullied your reputation," he finished.

"I enjoyed the dalliance. It's not like you forced me." His look darkened at her words, and Amanda realized she was making things worse instead of better. "I want you to know I release you from any sense of duty toward me. You know. The betrothal."

"I think I always knew I wasn't fit to marry. Or be around decent folk."

"You are decent folk, Bradley. Don't let anyone tell you any different."

"Easy for you to say. You were raised decent."

Amanda forced out a humorless laugh. "My father was an outlaw! You call that decent? Sure, Ma said he was going to give up the life. But was he really? I'll never know. Which means I've got thieving blood in my veins. Doesn't make me any less of a person than I always was."

"That girl, if she was my mother, was young and innocent. Hawkes raped her. And here I am, no better. Forced myself on you."

"No, Bradley. You were incapacitated and I took advantage of that fact. *I* forced myself on *you*. Sooner you settle on that fact, the better."

CHAPTER 11

Over the next six weeks Amanda and Laura made several trips into Yuma, visiting banks and lawyers and speaking on different occasions with the proprietor of the dance hall. Amanda felt they gleaned some very useful information and her project was starting to feel like more than some pipe dream. Both she and Laura had gotten over their amusement at the men's reactions to two women talking business. Eventually they stopped hearing, "... and will your husbands be joining us?"

"I'm so glad we're doing this." Laura patted her stomach. "Ever since I told Brody the news, he has been so smothering and protective, I feel like screaming some days." She cocked her head to where the twins rode beside them, one on each side. Brody refused to let her leave the ranch without at least two of the others accompanying her. "I'm like a prisoner in my own home. I fear it will only get worse once the baby comes."

Amanda sighed. "You're lucky you have someone who loves you and cares so much."

"I know. I have to say I am some disappointed you and

Bradley called things off. I was really looking forward to having another woman on the ranch."

"Braydon seems to find a lot of excuses to visit the house. Maybe he and Henny will make a match of it."

"Speaking of Henrietta, are they any closer to finding the famed ship of black pearls?"

"She and Percy seem pretty secretive. I'm guessing Hawkes is out as one of their investors, though." She turned. "Have you thought of investing in their quest? They're really impassioned."

"I thought about it," Laura said. "But it seems they want to do it on their own." She sighed. "Hawkes is still very much on Brody's mind."

Amanda fell silent. True to expectations, things had been smoothed over regarding Bradley's detainment and Hawkes's threats against her and Laura. She figured Brody and the others had their reasons to let things be for the time being.

As if privy to her thoughts, Laura added, "I'd give anything to know why Hawkes wants to control the Copper Moon Ranch so badly. There has to be more to it than a simple desire to thwart Brody and the others."

Amanda glanced over at Laura, whose hands rested on her still-flat stomach, and felt a fresh wave of guilt at deceiving her friend. Not for the first time, she considered calling off her plans to own a music hall in Bullet. How would Laura feel when she discovered the truth?

"The railway sure has changed things in Yuma," Laura said when they arrived in town. "I remember how quiet it was here when I was growing up."

Their little entourage pulled up in front of the Savings and Loan. Amanda hopped from the carriage first and turned to give Laura a hand. Abruptly, the bank's doors flew open. Bullets whizzed past her ear as she pushed Laura down onto the floor of the carriage and threw herself overtop of her. She heard shots exchanged close by and guessed the twins had joined in the fray.

The entire incident was over in seconds, with the thieves riding hellbent for the wind, closely followed by the sheriff and his deputy. As she slowly straightened, Amanda was aware of a searing pain in her right shoulder. She glanced over and saw a puddle of blood staining her gown.

She grasped the seat of the carriage as a wave of dizziness washed over her. She knew Laura and the twins were talking to her, but their words sounded far away. Her last coherent thought was that she'd never been one to faint at the slightest little thing before this year.

She woke in an unfamiliar bed with scratchy sheets. When she tried to move, she found her wrists restrained against the bed's side rails. The room had a strange, antiseptic smell. She blinked until, slowly, her vision cleared. Laura sat curled into a chair in one corner, where she appeared to be asleep.

As soon as Amanda moved and attempted to free her hands, Laura's eyes flew open, and she stood up. "Don't move. I'll call the nurse."

"Why are my hands tied down?"

"They didn't want you to roll around and rip out the stitches." Laura smiled down at her and brushed a strand of damp hair back from her forehead. "I think you might have saved my life."

Amanda made a face. "I don't know I'd go so far as to say that."

Just then the nurse arrived. "I thought I heard voices." She bustled in and untied Amanda's restraints before she picked up her wrist to check her pulse. "How are you feeling, my dear?"

"I want to go home," Amanda said crossly. "Hospitals are for sick people and I'm not sick."

"It's lucky, is what you are. You and your friend both. What's the world coming to? A bank robbery in broad daylight. Innocent folk getting shot." She tut-tutted as she fluffed Amanda's pillows. "You rest up. I'll see if I can find the doctor." The door closed softly behind her.

"I heard the doctor say if everything checks out, you can go home tomorrow," Laura said. "He just wants to make sure nothing happens to the baby because of the blood you lost." Her face softened. "Does anyone else know?"

Amanda shook her head and blinked back the well of tears threatening to leak from behind her eyelids. "I wasn't even really sure myself. I planned to tell you when I knew for sure. I just didn't ... " She paused and tried to draw a breath, but it hurt. "I didn't want anything to ruin our plans for the music hall."

"You'll need to tell Bradley eventually."

"I can't. He'll think it was deliberate. Another ploy to get him to marry me."

"Bradley won't think that. He's a good man, Amanda."

"He thinks Hawkes might be his father. How pleased will he be about another generation carrying that bloodline?"

"You can't do this alone."

"Of course I can. My mother raised me on her own. She didn't care what people said, and I don't either." Neither of them voiced the unspoken. Amanda's mother had at least been married to her father.

They were interrupted by a soft knock at the door. When Laura opened it, Amanda looked past her to where the twins hovered in the hall, seeming unsure if they should come in or wait outside.

"It's okay," Laura said. "She's awake." She bent over and gave Amanda a kiss on the brow. "These two are champing at the bit to get me back to the ranch before there's any more excitement today. But I couldn't leave until I knew you were okay."

Amanda swallowed thickly. She nodded and let her eyes drift closed. Lucky Laura. She had people who cared whether or not she made it home safely every day.

"We'll come by tomorrow morning and get you," Laura said. "I'll stop by the house first and pack you a clean gown. Any preferences?"

Amanda shook her head and turned her face away. She only turned back when she thought Laura had left, but her friend was still there, a concerned look on her face.

Amanda cleared her throat. "I'll be fine. You go home. I think getting shot at deserves some special pampering."

"So does saving someone's life."

Amanda forced a smile. "And I'm getting lots of rest and pampering here, aren't I?"

"I'll tell Brody what you said about my needing to be pampered." She paused. "Don't worry. That's all I'll tell him. Your story is yours to tell."

"Thank you," Amanda said softly to her friend's retreating back.

THINGS around the Copper Moon felt as near to normal as they ever got these days. The new herd of cattle the boys brought back from Mexico was thriving. Bradley was relieved Brody spent most of his free time fretting over

Laura's delicate condition, and his upcoming role as a father. Hawkes was keeping out of not just their way, but the towns-folk in general. Life in Bullet felt good. Which made it harder than ever to leave. Bradley hated good-byes.

Deliberately he waited till he knew the others were busy on the far reaches of the ranch to pack his things and saddle up. He was just fixing to mount Harley when Brody came bursting into the barn.

Bradley exhaled heavily. Brody stood at the entrance to the stall, disappointment pulling at his features. "This is how you plan to head off? Without a word to any of us? Your family, who were so worried about you. Who risked life and limb to see you back here safe."

Bradley stopped what he was doing and slowly turned to face the man he called "brother". "You all will be better off without me."

"How do you figure? Didn't we always say seven was our lucky number?"

"Hasn't felt so damn lucky lately," Bradley muttered.

"You're still alive, aren't you? Even after such a damn fool thing as chasing over to Hawkes's place by yourself. We all made an oath years ago. Sealed it in blood. We get him, but we do it right."

"There's lots you don't know."

"Not much happens around here I don't hear about one way or the other. I understand you said a few fool things to Barron when he was pulling you out of that dark hole."

"I was hit in the head. Don't rightly recall just what I might have been rambling on about."

Brody skewered him with a look. Bradley looked away, tightened the cinch on Haley's saddle. Checked that his bedroll was secure. Brody crossed his arms over his chest at the same time he crossed one booted foot over the other.

"Things are going to get even busier around here. Laura and I want to spend time with our young 'un after he comes. I'll need a second-in-command. Someone the others trust and respect."

"You've got Braydon for that."

"In case you haven't noticed, Braydon seems a tad distracted these days. And Blake tends to be too slow to kick some ass when it needs kicking."

Bradley straightened, faced Brody and squared his shoulders. "What are you trying to say, Brody? Don't go? My mind is made up. I'm not like the rest of you."

Brody was silent for a good long time before he spoke, almost as if he was weighing every word. "We've all got our pasts. I don't know what you took into your head about your parentage. Maybe it's a fact. Just as easy to think maybe it's not. Truth is, the only way a man can be a father is if he raises his young right, whether they fell from his seed or not. Hawkes? He was never anyone's father. That evil one you lived with? No father there. Old Gus at the circus? There was some right male influence. That man most likely saved your life in more ways than one."

Bradley looked down at his feet. A deep shame filled his belly and crawled up to lodge in his throat. "I kind of credit you with that. You and the others, whether you all know it or not."

"Making of a man has nothing to do with his blood. And everything to do with how he treats others."

"I haven't been treating folks all so shit hot these days."

"Like Amanda?" Brody said.

"Among others."

"Should be able to fix that. Might take some time. Might take some wooing."

"She won't want me. Not after everything I put her through."

"You might find yourself surprised. I put Laura through a fair bit, and she still kind of doesn't mind me." Brody said it with a wink and a grin, a grin Bradley couldn't help responding to. Laura worshipped the ground Brody walked on, same as him to her.

"Stay. Be an uncle to my young 'un. Help me and the boys do what we set out to do. Besides, there isn't anyone knows his way around our herd the way you do."

Bradley looked from his saddled mount to Brody, then back to his horse. He clapped Haley on the neck and the horse turned wise and soulful eyes his way. "Guess we're fixing ourselves to stay after all, buddy."

AMANDA WALKED out of Doc Parsons's office into Bullet's main thoroughfare. He'd checked over her shoulder and pronounced her fiddle-fit to start again doing things. Playing the piano and the like. Question was, what did she really want to do?

Laura was tired and staying back on the ranch more. Without her friend by her side, Amanda didn't have the confidence to plough ahead with the music hall, even though she'd secured the necessary financing to get the project rolling. The planning just didn't interest her like it had in the beginning.

She started to cross the street, making for the café, when she spotted him. Standing in the shadows of a cottonwood tree. His hat was pulled low on his forehead but she'd know that lanky build, that stubborn stance, anyplace. She raised her chin a notch and continued on her way. Bradley being here was not going to alter her plans one bit.

He caught up with her at the entrance to the café and held the door open for her.

"Thank you." She breezed in ahead and chose a table at the back, hardly expecting he would follow her.

"Mind if I join you?" He took off his hat and sat even before she answered.

"Why would I mind?" she said in what she hoped was a cool tone.

"Haven't seen you out at the ranch lately."

"I haven't been able to ride. Besides, struck me it would be easier that way. Without you and me bumping into each other, I mean."

"What did the doctor say?"

"I'm right as rain. Fiddle-fit."

He stared down at his clasped hands on the table top. "That was really brave what you did to protect Laura."

She shrugged. "Anyone would have done the same."

He looked up, skewered her with that ink-black gaze of his that never gave away a thing. "I can tell she misses you. Maybe now that you can ride again, you won't be such a stranger."

Amanda was aware of her feet doing their own little dance beneath the table, as if sitting still was suddenly too much. "I miss her too. Tell her I'll be along one of these days." She looked up at him. "Is that it? Is that what you came to say?"

"I never got a chance to thank you proper. You were the one knew to go to the circus and get things figured out from there."

"You're welcome." She saw Georgina hovering, unsure

147

whether to approach the table or not and gave her a quick nod.

"Howdy, Bradley. Amanda. Coffee?"

Amanda was already finding her stomach felt queasy at the smell of cooking eggs and brewing coffee. The doctor had warned her that might happen. "I'll have a cup of tea, please."

"Black coffee for me," Bradley said. "Thank you, Georgina."

The silence lengthened as their beverages arrived and she added cream and sugar to hers.

Bradley cleared his throat several times in a way that told Amanda he had more on his mind.

"Laura said you'd been thinking on starting a music hall. Something like that one we saw in Yuma when you and I were there."

She blew on her tea. "Thinking on it."

"Laura kinda said, since she's not really able to get involved too much in the planning right now, maybe I could... Maybe I step in and take her place. If you'd like that."

Amanda narrowed her gaze. "Why would you want to do that?"

Bradley heaved a sigh. Ran a hand through his straight black hair. "I'm not saying this well. Laura's not the only one who misses you. I thought maybe we could spend some time together. Be company for each other."

Amanda pushed her chair back and got to her feet. "Bradley Mason, I swear you are the most obtuse man I ever met." With that, she gathered her reticule, turned on her heel and left him sitting there.

Bradley looked up as Georgina approached with the coffee pot. "What's obtuse mean?"

"Thick-headed and stupid. Like most of your tribe. What're you doing just sitting there? Go after her!"

Amanda was nearly home before Bradley caught up to her. She heard him behind her calling her name but just kept walking. Right up to the point where he grabbed her arm and spun her around to face him before he pulled her into his arms.

"You're right. I am thick-headed and stubborn and just about any other name you can think to throw at me. I'm also crazy in love with you and miss you something awful. The dance hall was just an excuse to spend time with you. To find out if maybe one day you could love me back."

Slowly, Amanda relaxed against him. "You needed an excuse?"

"I thought I did. Hoped one day, if things worked out, maybe I could ask you proper to marry me, instead of just throwing it out the way I did before. I've got a lot to learn about wooing a woman. Braydon has been giving me pointers, but how can I practice if I never see you?"

She widened her eyes, drew back in his arms so she could look directly at him. "What kind of pointers has Braydon been giving you?"

His slow, sure smile warmed her insides right down to the soles of her feet, the same way it always had. "Invite me inside. That way I can show you first hand."

"Percy and Henrietta will be there."

"Then they better get used to me hanging around here a lot." As he spoke, he lowered his head toward hers. She waited impatiently for his kiss, but he took his time. First there were licks and nibbles and sips against the side of her neck that sent her into a near-swoon as his hands tightened on her waist.

Finally, his lips claimed hers and sealed their future

with a sure, slow kiss that promised her his heart, his soul, his life and beyond.

Theirs was a very short betrothal, sped along by the words Amanda eventually whispered in his ear with much trepidation. She'd been worried how he might take the news, but after his initial shock and disbelief, Bradley could be seen beaming ear-to-ear, hurrying his brothers along in the construction of a home on the ranch for him and his new bride.

THE ARIZONA SUN shone brightly overhead, raining its golden sheen on the church bell tower as it peeled its happy news throughout the entire town of Bullet. The church bells faded away to be replaced by the familiar notes of the bridal march.

From her place at the back of the church Amanda watched her matron of honor Laura, in a dress designed to camouflage her condition, make her way slowly down the aisle to the altar, where the groom waited alongside his brothers.

Amanda silently counted Laura's steps until it was her turn to walk toward her love and into their future. Brody had offered to give her away, but she had elected to do this alone, one last thing she would be doing on her own. Besides, Bradley should have all of his brothers next to him.

Head high, eyes straight ahead, she took a breath and began to walk slowly toward the front of the church where Bradley stood, his brothers lined in a neat and serious row to his left.

Like they'd practiced, he met her half-way across the floor in front of the altar and took her hand in his. Together they moved to where the reverend waited. Amanda smiled at her love from behind the veil she wore. The same veil her mother had worn the day she married Amanda's father.

The small church was all but bursting at the seams, for the entire town was on hand to witness the joining of their beloved pianist to one of the Mason brothers. There were a few murmured speculations among the guests as to which brother would be the next one to get hitched.

From her seat in the second pew, Henrietta stirred restlessly, unable to tear her gaze from one particular dark and handsome brother, Braydon Mason. She didn't wish to have her gaze drawn that way. Had no intention of being distracted from the project that had brought her to Bullet in the first place. Still, something about Braydon stirred her senses and triggered feelings she had long thought lost forever.

Thanks for reading *Bradley's Bride*. You might not know how important reader reviews are, but they mean a lot. Just a short sentence saying you enjoyed the book goes a long way with new readers and puts a smile on this author's face.

Review wherever your purchased *Bradley's Bride* or on Goodreads or BookBub.

And please keep in touch

Website: KathleenLawless.com
Facebook: facebook.com/kathleenlawlessnovels
Instagram: instagram.com/kathleenflawless
TikTok: tiktok.com/@kathleenflawless

If you haven't already done so, sign up for my VIP Reader's Newsletter and be the first to hear about free books, fan-priced sales, and my new series. http://eepurl.com/bVosb1

Keep reading for a preview of Seven Brides for Seven Brothers, book 3, *Braydon's Bride*.

Dear Reader

The American West in the last half of the nineteenth century offers my heroines a chance to assert their independence and also introduce them to a hero who is their match in every way. My characters have their own ideas of right and wrong, good versus evil, and deal with it on their terms. It wasn't called the Wild West for nothing. Life was about conquest, survival and persistence,

I love writing a historical genre where the reader, by the simple act of picking up the book, instantly suspends disbelief. She easily forgets about her world and her woes in a tale where no one needs to empty the dishwasher or take out the trash, and adventure lies around every corner.

As an author, it's fun to carry her away to a time and place where anything could, and often did, happen. The customs of the day and the manner of dress might be different from today's world, but people are still people. They laugh, love, hurt and heal. Celebrate and mourn. They live life large. And in the untamed wildness of the settling of the west anything can happen.

Read on for an excerpt from Book 3, *Braydon's Bride*.

BRAYDON'S BRIDE - EXCERPT
Copyright ©2019 Kathleen Lawless

Henrietta heaved a sigh of relief as Braydon sauntered back to the bride and groom's head table. "Don't encourage him," she hissed under her breath to her friend, Percy.

Percy shook his elegant blond head. "Darling, Henny. Men like Braydon Mason don't need encouragement. They thrive on any sort of challenge."

Henrietta sniffed. "As long as he doesn't consider me one. I was warned he fancies himself quite the ladies' man. He was raised in a brothel, of all places."

Percy laughed out loud, causing a few of the guests to look their way, wondering if they had missed a good joke. "I don't know if I ought to envy the bloke or pity him. Oops, don't look now, but here he comes."

Sure enough, Henrietta looked up to see Braydon making a bee-line for their table. She rose before he reached them, scanning the room for the nearest exit, but only made it two steps before he caught her arm. She glanced back, horrified to see he held her shawl and her reticule in one large, sun-browned hand.

"Forgetting something?"

There was no mistaking the teasing glint in his dark eyes. She tossed her head proudly. "Not at all. I was just ..." She glanced around, seeking an excuse for her attempt to flee. "I was just going for another glass of Champagne."

"Great idea. I could use a beer." Before she knew it, her hand was tucked in the crook of his arm, and secured there with his free hand. The warmth of his clasp sent unwanted tingles of awareness up her arm and beyond.

Henrietta felt the curious gaze from more than a few

pairs of eyes following their progress, and much as she wanted to pull away and tell Braydon Mason to keep his filthy hands to himself, she reminded herself there was a time and a place for everything. She was the newcomer here, and something of a curiosity to the locals.

"'Nuther beer, Bray?" the bartender greeted him.

"And Champagne for the lady, Mac."

"Coming right up."

"Thank you," she said, accepting the glass Braydon held her way, relieved when he released her to pick up their drinks from the bar.

"My pleasure." The way he watched her over the rim of his glass implied his pleasures were vast and varied. And that he wasn't above sharing.

Two could play at that game!

She leaned against the bar, not taking her eyes from him. "I hear the women in town are all wondering who will be the next Mason brother down the aisle, and with which lucky lady."

"I've got four other brothers in the running. I'll sit that race out."

"Don't be saying that too loudly," Henrietta said. "I can't bear the sight of female tears."

"One more thing we have in common."

"I wasn't aware we had anything in common, Mr. Mason."

"I told you. Braydon." He reached forward and tucked a loose strand of hair behind her ear with an easily familiarity that annoyed her. She went to bat his hand away, but he caught her hand in his and raised it to his mouth. Before she could jerk free his tongue made the most delicious warm, hot swirls across her palm at the same time his thumb stroked the sensitive underside of her wrist.

Pulling her hand away was the furthest thing from her mind.

Instead, she dashed her glass of Champagne in his face.

～

Get your copy of *Braydon's Bride* today or keep reading to see more books by Kathleen.

Mail Order Noelle

Chelsea's Choice

Lila: Rescue Me Mail Order Brides

Here Come the Brides Volume 1

Here Come the Brides Volume 2

Sweet Contemporary Romance

Frannie (Always a Bridesmaid)

Baxter (Last Man Standing)

Blue Sky Island

One Cinderella Spring

One Stolen Summer

One Fantasy Fall

One Wondrous Winter

Sweet Christmas Romance Novellas

Holly's Wish

No Groom at the Inn

Steamy Contemporary Romance

SECRET SEDUCTIONS

Her Untamed Cowboy - Book 1

Her Undercover Cowboy - Book 2

Her Unwilling Cowboy - Book 3

Who Needs a Cowboy! - Book 4

Intimate Strangers

Steamy Historical Romance

Taboo

Unmasked

Reckless Rogues - Box Set of the 2 Books

Romantic Suspense

Final Heat

Afterburn

Women's Fiction

Fabulous at Fifty

For a complete book list visit KathleenLawless.com

To be the first to hear about Kathleen's new releases, special fan pricing sales, and also receive a free book, sign up for her VIP Reader Newsletter at http://eepurl.com/bVosbI

ABOUT THE AUTHOR

USA Today Bestselling Author, Kathleen Lawless, blames a misspent youth watching Rawhide, Maverick and Bonanza for her fascination with cowboys, which doesn't stop her from creating a wide variety of interests and occupations for her many alpha male heroes.

With nearly 50 published novels to her credit, she enjoys pushing the boundaries of traditional romance into historical romance, contemporary romance, romantic suspense and women's fiction.

She makes her home in the Pacific Northwest and loves to hear from her readers.

Sign up for Kathleen's VIP Reader Newsletter to receive updates, special giveaways and fan-priced offers. http:// eepurl.com/bVosb1

KathleenLawless.com
Goodreads | BookBub
Facebook | Instagram | TikTok

amazon.com/Kathleen-Lawless/e/B001IXS2SA

goodreads.com/kathleenlawless

bookbub.com/authors/kathleen-lawless

facebook.com/kathleenlawlessnovels

instagram.com/kathleenflawless

tiktok.com/@kathleenflawless